Winter Roses

**Center Point
Large Print**

**This Large Print Book carries the
Seal of Approval of N.A.V.H.**

Winter Roses

DIANA PALMER

CENTER POINT PUBLISHING
THORNDIKE, MAINE

This Center Point Large Print edition
is published in the year 2008 by arrangement with
Harlequin Books S.A.

The text of this Large Print edition is unabridged. In other
aspects, this book may vary from the original edition.
Printed in the United States of America.
Set in 16-point Times New Roman type.

ISBN: 978-1-60285-112-2

Library of Congress Cataloging-in-Publication Data

Palmer, Diana.
    Winter roses / Diana Palmer.--Center Point large print ed.
        p. cm.
    ISBN 978-1-60285-112-2 (lib. bdg. : alk. papcr)
    1. Ranchers--Fiction. 2. Young women--Fiction. 3. Female friendship--Fiction. 4. Texas--
Fiction. 5. Large type books. I. Title.

    PS3566.A513W55 2008
    813'.54--dc22

2007048762

CHAPTER ONE

IT WAS late, and Ivy was going to miss her class. Rachel was the only person, except Ivy's best friend, who even knew the number of Ivy's frugal prepaid cell phone. The call had come just as she was going to her second college class of the day. The argument could have waited until the evening, but her older sister never thought of anyone's convenience. Well, except her own, that was.

"Rachel, I'm going to be late," Ivy pleaded into the phone. She pushed back a strand of long, pale blond hair. Her green eyes darkened with worry. "And we've got a test today!"

"I don't care what you've got," her older sister snapped. "You just listen to me. I want that check for Dad's property, as soon as you can get the insurance company to issue it! I've got overdue bills and you're whining about college classes. It's a waste of money! Aunt Hettie should never have left you that savings account," she added angrily. "It should have been mine, too. I'm the oldest."

She was, and she'd taken everything she could get her hands on, anything she could pawn for ready cash. Ivy had barely been able to keep enough to pay the funeral bills when they came due. It was a stroke of luck that Aunt Hettie had liked her and had left her a small inheritance. Perhaps she'd realized that Ivy would be lucky if she was able to keep so much as a penny of their father's few assets.

It was the same painful argument they'd had for a solid month, since their father had died of a stroke. Ivy had been left with finding a place to live while Rachel called daily to talk to the attorney who was probating the will. All she wanted was the money. She'd coaxed their father into changing his will, so that she got everything when he died.

Despite the fact that he paid her little attention, Ivy was still grieving. She'd taken care of their father while he was dying from the stroke. He'd thought that Rachel was an angel. All their lives, it had been Rachel who got all the allowances, all the inherited jewelry—which Rachel pawned immediately—all the attention. Ivy was left with housework and yardwork and cooking for the three of them. It hadn't been much of a life. Her rare dates had been immediately captivated by Rachel, who took pleasure in stealing them away from her younger, plainer sister, only to drop them days later. When Rachel had opted to go to New York and break into theater, their father had actually put a lien on his small house to pay for an apartment for her. It had meant budgeting to the bone and no new dresses for Ivy. When she tried to protest the unequal treatment the sisters received, their father said that Ivy was just jealous and that Rachel needed more because she was beautiful but emotionally challenged.

Translated, that meant Rachel had no feelings for anyone except herself. But Rachel had convinced their father that she adored him, and she'd filled his ears with lies about Ivy, right up to accusing her of sneaking out at night to meet men and stealing from the garage where she worked two evenings a week keeping books. No protest was enough to convince him that Ivy was honest, and that she didn't even attract many men. She never could keep a prospective boyfriend once they saw Rachel.

"If I can learn bookkeeping, I'll have a way to support myself, Rachel," Ivy said quietly.

"You could marry a rich man one day, I guess, if you could find a blind one," Rachel conceded, and laughed at her little joke. "Although where you expect to find one in Jacobsville, Texas, is beyond me."

"I'm not looking for a husband. I'm in school at our community vocational college," Ivy reminded her.

"So you are. What a pitiful future you're heading for." Rachel paused to take an audible sip of her drink. "I've got two auditions tomorrow. One's for the lead in a new play, right on Broadway. Jerry says I'm a shoo-in. He has influence with the director."

Ivy wasn't usually sarcastic, but Rachel was getting on her nerves. "I thought Jerry didn't want you to work."

There was a frigid pause on the other end of the line. "Jerry doesn't mind it," she said coolly. "He just likes me to stay in, so that he can take care of me."

"He feeds you uppers and downers and crystal meth and charges you for the privilege, you mean," Ivy replied quietly. She didn't add that Rachel was beautiful and that Jerry probably used her as bait to catch new clients. He took her to party after party. She talked about acting, but it was only talk. She could barely remember her own name when she was on drugs, much less remember lines for a play. She drank to excess as well, just like Jerry.

"Jerry takes care of me. He knows all the best people in theater. He's promised to introduce me to one of the angels who's producing that new comedy. I'm going to make it to Broadway or die trying," Rachel said curtly. "And if we're going to argue, we might as well not even speak!"

"I'm not arguing . . ."

"You're putting Jerry down, all the time!"

Ivy felt as if she were standing on a precipice, looking at the bottom of the world. "Have you really forgotten what Jerry did to me?" she asked, recalling the one visit Rachel had made home, just after their father died. It had been an overnight one, with the insufferable Jerry at her side. Rachel had signed papers to have their father cremated, placing his ashes in the grave with those of his late wife, the girls' mother. It was rushed and unpleasant, with Ivy left grieving alone for a parent who'd never loved her, who'd treated her very badly. Ivy had a big, forgiving heart. Rachel did manage a sniff into a handkerchief at the graveside service. But her eyes weren't either wet or red. It was an act, as it always was with her.

"What you said he did," came the instant, caustic reply. "Jerry said he never gave you any sort of drugs!"

"Rachel!" she exclaimed, furious now, "I wouldn't

lie about something like that! I had a migraine and he switched my regular medicine with a powerful narcotic. When I saw what he was trying to give me, I threw them at him. He thought I was too sick to notice. He thought it would be funny if he could make me into an addict, just like you . . . !'"

"Oh, grow up," Rachel shouted. "I'm no addict! Everybody uses drugs! Even people in that little hick town where you live. How do you think I used to score before I moved to New York? There was always somebody dealing, and I knew where to find what I needed. You're so naive, Ivy."

"My brain still works," she shot back.

"Watch your mouth, kid," Rachel said angrily, "or I'll see that you don't get a penny of Dad's estate."

"Don't worry, I never expected to get any of it," Ivy said quietly. "You convinced Daddy that I was no good, so that he wouldn't leave me anything."

"You've got that pittance from Aunt Hettie," Rachel repeated. "Even though I should have had it. I deserved it, having to live like white trash all those years when I was at home."

"Rachel, if you got what you really deserved," Ivy replied with a flash of bravado, "you'd be in federal prison."

There was a muffled curse. "I have to go. Jerry's back. Listen, you check with that lawyer and find out what's the holdup. I can't afford all these long-distance calls."

"You never pay for them. You usually reverse the

charges when you call me," she was reminded.

"Just hurry up and get the paperwork through so you can send me my check. And don't expect me to call you back until you're ready to talk like an adult instead of a spoiled kid with a grudge!"

The receiver slammed down in her ear. She folded it back up with quiet resignation. Rachel would never believe that Jerry, her knight in shining armor, was nothing more than a sick little social climbing drug dealer with a felony record who was holding her hostage to substance abuse. Ivy had tried for the past year to make her older sibling listen, but she couldn't. The two of them had never been close, but since Rachel got mixed up with Jerry, and hooked on meth, she didn't seem capable of reason anymore. In the old days, even when Rachel was being difficult, she did seem to have some small affection for her sister. That all changed when she was a junior in high school. Something had happened, Ivy had never known what, that turned her against Ivy and made a real enemy of her. Alcohol and drug use hadn't helped Rachel's already abrasive personality. It had been an actual relief for Ivy when her sister left for New York just days after the odd blowup. But it seemed that she could cause trouble long-distance, whenever she liked.

Ivy went down the hall quickly to her next class, without any real enthusiasm. She didn't want to spend her life working for someone else, but she certainly didn't want to go to New York and end up as Rachel's maid and cook, as she had been before her sister left

Jacobsville. Letting Rachel have their inheritance would be the easier solution to the problem. Anything was better than having to live with Rachel again; even having to put up with Merrie York's brother, Stuart, in order to have one true friend.

It was Friday, and when she left the campus for home, riding with her fellow boarder, Lita Dawson, who taught at the vocational college, she felt better. She'd passed her English test, she was certain of it. But typing was getting her down. She couldn't manage more than fifty words a minute to save her life. One of the male students typing with both index fingers could do it faster than Ivy could.

They pulled up in front of the boardinghouse where they both lived. Ivy felt absolutely drained. She'd had to leave her father's house because she couldn't even afford to pay the light bill. Besides, Rachel had signed papers to put the house on the market the same day she'd signed the probate papers at a local lawyer's office. Since Ivy wasn't old enough, at almost nineteen, to handle the legal affairs, Rachel had charmed the new, young attorney handling the probate and convinced him that Ivy needed looking after, preferably in a boardinghouse. Then she'd flown back to New York, leaving Ivy to dip into a great-aunt's small legacy and a part-time job as a bookkeeper at a garage on Monday and Thursday evenings to pay for her board and the small student fee that Texas residents paid at the state technical and vocational college. Rachel hadn't even asked if Ivy had enough to live on.

Merrie had tried to get Stuart to help Ivy fight Rachel's claim on the bulk of the estate, but Ivy almost had hysterics when she offered. She'd rather have lived in a cardboard box by the side of the road than have Stuart take over her life. She didn't want to tell her best friend that her brother terrified her. Merrie would have asked why. There were secrets in Ivy's past that she shared with no one.

"I'm going to see my father this weekend." Lita, dark-haired and eyed, smiled at the younger woman. "How about you?"

Ivy smiled. "If Merrie remembers, we'll probably go window-shopping." She sighed, smiling lazily. "I might see something I can daydream about owning," she chuckled.

"One day some nice man is going to come along and treat you the way you deserve to be treated," Lita said kindly. "You wait and see."

Ivy knew better, but she only smiled. She wasn't anxious to offer any man control of her life. She was through living in fear.

She went in the side door, glancing over to see if Mrs. Brown was home. The landlady must be grocery shopping, she decided. It was a Friday ritual. Ivy got to eat with Mrs. Brown and Lita Dawson, the other tenant, on the weekends. She and Lita took turns cooking and cleaning up the kitchen, to help elderly Mrs. Brown manage the extra work. It was nice, not having to drive into town to get a sandwich. The pizza place delivered, but Ivy was sick of pizza. She liked her small boardinghouse, and Lita was nice, if a little older than Ivy. Lita was newly divorced and missing her ex-husband to a terrible degree. She fell back on her degree and taught computer technology at the vocational college, and let Ivy ride back and forth with her for help with the gas money.

She'd no sooner put down her purse than the cell phone rang.

"It's the weekend!" came a jolly, laughing voice. It was Merrie York, her best friend from high school.

"I noticed," Ivy chuckled. "How'd you do on your tests?"

"I'm sure I passed something, but I'm not sure what. My biology final is approaching and lab work is killing me. I can't make the microscope work!"

"You're training to be a nurse, not a lab assistant," Ivy pointed out.

"Come up here and tell that to my biology professor," Merrie dared her. "Never mind, I'll graduate even if I have to take every course three times."

"That's the spirit."

"Come over and spend the weekend with me," Merrie invited.

Ivy's heart flipped over. "Thanks, but I have some things to do around here . . ."

"He's in Oklahoma, settling a new group of cattle with a sale barn," Merrie coaxed wryly.

Ivy hesitated. "Can you put that in writing and get it notarized?"

"He really likes you, deep inside."

"He's made an art of hiding his fondness for me," Ivy shot back. "I love you, Merrie, but I don't fancy being cannon fodder. It's been a long week. Rachel and I had another argument today."

"Long distance?"

"Exactly."

"And over Sir Lancelot the drug lord."

"You know me too well."

Merrie laughed. "We've been friends since middle school," she reminded Ivy.

"Yes, the debutante and the tomboy. What a pair we made."

"You're not quite the tomboy you used to be," Merrie said.

"We conform when we have to. Why do you want me there this weekend?"

"For selfish reasons," the other woman said mischievously. "I need a study partner and everybody else in my class has a social life."

"I don't want a social life," Ivy said. "I want to make good grades and graduate and get a job that pays at least minimum wage."

"Your folks left you a savings account and some stocks," Merrie pointed out.

That was true, but Rachel had walked away with most of the money and all of the stocks.

"Your folks left you Stuart," Ivy replied dryly.

"Don't remind me!"

"Actually, I suppose it was the other way around,

14

wasn't it?" Ivy thought aloud. "Your folks left you to Stuart."

"He's a really great brother," Merrie said gently. "And he likes most women . . ."

"He likes all women, except me," Ivy countered. "I really couldn't handle a weekend with Stuart right now. Not on top of being harassed by Rachel and final exams."

"You're a whiz at math," her friend countered. "You hardly ever have to study."

"Translation—I work math problems every day for four hours after class so that I can appear to be smart."

Merrie laughed. "Come on over. Mrs. Rhodes is making homemade yeast rolls for supper, and we have all the pay per view channels. We can study and then watch that new adventure movie."

Ivy was weakening. On weekends, it was mostly takeout at the boardinghouse. Ivy's stomach rebelled at the thought of pizza or more sweet and sour chicken or tacos. "I could really use an edible meal that didn't come in a box, I guess."

"If I tell Mrs. Rhodes you're coming, she'll make you a cherry pie."

"That does it. I'll pack a nightgown and see you in thirty minutes, or as soon as I can get a cab."

"I could come and get you."

"No. Cabs are cheap in town. I'm not destitute," she added proudly, although she practically was. The cab fare would have to come out of her snack money for the next week. She really did have to budget to the bone. But her pride wouldn't let her accept Merrie's offer.

"All right, Miss Independence. I'll have Jack leave the gate open."

It was a subtle and not arrogant reminder that the two women lived in different social strata. Merrie's home was a sprawling brick mansion with a wrought-iron gate running up a bricked driveway. There was an armed guard, Jack, at the front gate, miles of electrified fence and two killer Dobermans who had the run of the property at night. If that didn't deter trespassers, there were the ranch hands, half of whom were ex-military. Stuart was particular about the people who worked for him, because his home contained priceless inherited antiques. He also owned four herd sires who commanded incredible stud fees; straws of their semen sold for thousands of dollars each and were shipped all over the world.

"Should I wear body armor, or will Chayce recognize me?"

Chayce McLeod was the chief of security for York Properties, which Stuart headed. He'd worked for J.B. Hammock, but Stuart had offered him a bigger salary and fringe benefits. Chayce was worth it. He had a degree in management and he was a past master at handling men. There were plenty of them to handle on a spread this size. Most people didn't know that Chayce was also an ex-federal agent. He was dishy, too, but Ivy was immune to him.

Stuart's ranch, all twenty thousand acres of it, was

only a part of an empire that spanned three states and included real estate, investments, feedlots and a ranching equipment company. Stuart and Merrie were very rich. But neither of them led a frantic social life. Stuart worked on the ranch, just as he had when he was in his teens—just as his father had until he died of a heart attack when Merrie was thirteen. Now, Stuart was thirty. Merrie, like Ivy, was only eighteen, almost nineteen. There were no other relatives. Their mother had died giving birth to Merrie.

Merrie sighed at the long pause. "Of course Chayce will recognize you. Ivy, you're not in one of your moods again, are you?"

"My dad was a mechanic, Merrie," she reminded her friend, "and my mother was a C.P.A. in a firm."

"My grandfather was a gambler who got lucky down in the Caribbean," Merrie retorted. "He was probably a closet pirate, and family legend says he was actually arrested for arms dealing when he was in his sixties. That's where our money came from. It certainly didn't come from hard work and honest living. Our parents instilled a vicious work ethic in both of us, as you may have noticed. We don't just sit around sipping mint juleps and making remarks about the working class. Now will you just shut up and start packing?"

Ivy laughed. "Okay. I'll see you shortly."

"That's my buddy."

Ivy had to admit that neither Merrie nor Stuart could ever be accused of resting on the family fortune. Stuart was always working on the ranch, when he wasn't flying to the family corporation's board meetings or meeting with legislators on agricultural bills or giving workshops on new facets of the beef industry. He had a degree from Yale in business, and he spoke Spanish fluently. He was also the most handsome, sensuous, attractive man Ivy had ever known. It took a lot of work for her to pretend that he didn't affect her. It was self-defense. Stuart preferred tall, beautiful, independent blondes, preferably rich ones. He was vocal about marriage, which he abhorred. His women came and went. Nobody lasted more than six months.

But Ivy was plain and soft-spoken, not really an executive sort of woman even if she'd been older than she was. She lived in a world far removed from Stuart's, and his friends intimidated her. She didn't know a certificate of deposit from a treasury bond, and her background didn't include yearly trips to exotic places. She didn't read literary fiction, listen to classical music, drive a luxury car or go shopping in boutiques. She lived a quiet life, working and studying hard to provide a future for herself. Merrie was in nursing school in San Antonio, where she lived in the dorm and drove a new Mercedes. The two only saw each other when Merrie came home for the occasional weekend. Ivy missed her.

That was why she took a chance and packed her bag. Merrie wouldn't lie to her about Stuart being there, she knew. But he frequently turned up unexpectedly. It wasn't surprising that he disliked Ivy. He'd known her sister, Rachel, before she went to New York. He was scathing about her lifestyle, which had been extremely modern even when she was still in high school. He thought Ivy was going to be just like her. Which proved that he didn't know his sister's best friend in the least.

Jack, the guard on the front gate at Merrie's house, recognized Ivy in the local cab, and grinned at her. He waved the cab through without even asking for any identification. One hurdle successfully passed, she told herself.

Merrie was waiting for her at the front steps of the sprawling brick mansion. She ran down the steps and around to the back door of the cab, throwing her arms around Ivy the minute she opened the door and got out.

Ivy was medium height and slender, with long, straight, pale blond hair and green eyes. Merrie took after her brother—she was tall for a woman, and she had dark hair and light eyes. She towered over Ivy.

"I'm so glad you came," Merrie said happily. "Sometimes the walls just close in on me when I'm here alone. The house is way too big for two people and a housekeeper."

"Both of you will marry someday and fill it up with kids," Ivy teased.

"Fat chance, in Stuart's case," Merrie chuckled. "Come on in. Where's your bag?"

"In the boot . . ."

The Hispanic driver was already at the trunk, smiling as he lifted out Ivy's bag and carried it all the way up to the porch for her. But before Ivy could reach into her purse, Merrie pressed a big bill into the driver's hand

and spoke to him in her own, elegant Spanish.

Ivy started to argue, but the cab was racing down the driveway and Merrie was halfway up the front steps.

"Don't argue," she told Ivy with a grin. "You know you can't win."

"I know," the other woman sighed. "Thanks, Merrie, but . . ."

"But you've got about three dollars spare a week, and you'd do without lunch one day at school to pay for the cab," came the quiet reply. "If you were in my place, you'd do it for me," she added, and Ivy couldn't argue. But it did hurt her pride.

"Listen," Merrie added, "one day when you're a fabulously rich owner of a bookkeeping firm, and driving a Rolls, you can pay me back. Okay?"

Ivy just laughed. "Listen, no C.P.A. ever got rich enough to own a Rolls," came the dry reply. "But I really will pay you back."

"Friends help friends," Merrie said simply. "Come on in."

The house was huge, really huge. The one thing that set rich people apart from poor people, Ivy pondered, was space. If you were wealthy, you could afford plenty of room in your house and a bathroom the size of a garage. You could also afford enough land to give you some privacy and a place to plant flowers and trees and have a fish pond . . .

"What are you brooding about now?" Merrie asked on the way up the staircase.

"Space," Ivy murmured.

"Outer?"

"No. Personal space," Ivy qualified the answer. "I was thinking that how much space you have depends on how much money you have. I'd love to have just a yard. And maybe a fish pond," she added.

"You can feed our Chinese goldfish any time you want to," the other girl offered.

Ivy didn't reply. She noticed, not for the first time, how much Merrie resembled her older brother. They were both tall and slender, with jet-black hair. Merrie wore her hair long, but Stuart's was short and conventionally cut. Her eyes, pale blue like Stuart's, could take on a steely, dangerous quality when she was angry. Not that Merrie could hold a candle to Stuart in a temper. Ivy had seen grown men hide in the barn when he passed by. Stuart's pale, deep-set eyes weren't the only indication of bad temper. His walk was just as good a measure of ill humor. He usually glided like a runner. But when he was angry, his walk slowed. The slower the walk, the worse the temper.

Ivy had learned early in her friendship with Merrie to see how fast Stuart was moving before she approached any room he was in. One memorable day when he'd lost a prize cattle dog to a coyote, she actually pleaded a migraine headache she didn't have to avoid sitting at the supper table with him.

It was a nasty habit of his to be bitingly sarcastic to anyone within range when he was mad, especially if the object of his anger was out of reach.

Merrie led Ivy into the bedroom that adjoined hers and watched as Ivy opened the small bag and brought out a clean pair of jeans and a cotton T-shirt. She frowned. "No nightgown?"

Ivy winced. "Rachel upset me. I forgot."

"No problem. You can borrow one of mine. It will drag the floor behind you like a train, of course, but it will fit most everywhere else." Her eyes narrowed. "I suppose Rachel is after the money."

Ivy nodded, looking down into her small bag. "She was good at convincing Daddy I didn't deserve anything."

"She told lies."

Ivy nodded again. "But he believed her. Rachel could be so sweet and loving when she wanted something. He drank . . ." She stopped at once.

Merrie sat down on the bed and folded her hands in her lap. "I know he drank, Ivy," she said gently. "Stuart had him investigated."

Her eyes widened in disbelief. "What?"

Merrie bit her lower lip. "I can't tell you why, so don't even ask. Suffice it to say that it was an eye-opening experience."

Ivy wondered how much information Stuart's private detective had ferreted out about the private lives of the Conley family.

"We just knew that he drank," Merrie said at once, when she saw her friend's tortured expression. She patted Ivy's hand. "Nobody has that perfect childhood they put in motion pictures, you know. Dad wanted

Stuart to raise thoroughbreds to race in competition. It was something he'd never been able to do. He tried to force Stuart through agricultural college." She laughed hollowly. "Nobody could force my brother to do anything, not even Dad."

"Were they very much alike?" Ivy asked, because she'd only met the elder York a few times.

"No. Well, in one way they were," she corrected. "Dad in a bad temper could cost us good hired men. Stuart cost us our best, and oldest, horse wrangler last week."

"How?"

"He made a remark Stuart didn't like when Stuart ran the Jaguar through the barn and into its back wall."

CHAPTER TWO

IVY could hardly contain her amusement. Merrie's brother was one of the most self-contained people she'd ever known. He never lost control of himself. "Stuart ran the Jag through the barn? The new Jaguar, the XJ?"

Merrie grimaced. "I'm afraid so. He was talking on his cell phone at the time."

"About what, for heaven's sake?"

"One of the managers at the Jacobsville sales barn mixed up the lot numbers and sold Stuart's purebred cows, all of whom were pregnant by Big Blue, for the price of open heifers," she added, the term "open heifer" denoting a two-year-old female who wasn't pregnant. Big Blue was a champion Black Angus herd sire.

"That was an expensive mistake," Ivy commented.

"And not only for us," Merrie added, tongue-in-cheek. "Stuart took every cattle trailer we had and every one he could borrow, complete with drivers, went to the sale barn and brought back every single remaining bull or cow or calf he was offering for sale. Then he shipped them to another sale barn in Oklahoma by train. That's why he's in Oklahoma. He said this time, they're going to be certain which lots they're selling at which price, because he's having it written on their hides in magic marker."

Ivy just grinned. She knew Stuart would do no such thing, even if he felt like it.

"The local sale barn is never going to be the same," Merrie added. "Stuart told them they'd be having snowball fights in hell before he sent another lot of cattle to them for an auction."

"Your brother is not a forgiving person," Ivy said quietly.

The other girl nodded. "But there's a reason for the way he is, Ivy," she said. "Our father expected Stuart to follow in his footsteps and become a professional athlete. Dad never made it out of semipro football, but he was certain that Stuart would. He started making him play football before he was even in grammar school. Stuart hated it," she recalled sadly. "He deliberately missed practices, and when he did, Dad would go at him with a doubled-up belt. Stuart had bruises all over his back and legs, but it made him that much more determined to avoid sports. When he was thirteen, he dug his heels in and told Dad he was going into rodeo and that if the belt came out again, he was going to call Dallas Carson and have him arrested for beating him. Dallas," she reminded Ivy, "was Hayes Carson's father. He was our sheriff long before Hayes went into law enforcement. It was unusual for someone to be arrested for spanking a child twenty years ago, but Dallas would have done it. He loved Stuart like a son."

It took Ivy a minute to answer. She knew more about corporal punishment than she was ever going to admit, even to Merrie. "I always liked Dallas. Hayes is hard-going sometimes. What did your father say to that?" she asked.

"He didn't say anything. He got Stuart in the car and drove him to football practice. Five minutes after he left, Stuart hitched a ride to the Jacobsville rodeo arena and borrowed a horse for the junior bulldogging competition. He and his best friend, Martin, came in second place. Dad was livid. When Stuart put his trophy on the mantel, Dad smashed it with a fire poker. He never took the belt to Stuart again, but he browbeat him and demeaned him every chance he got. It wasn't until Stuart went away to college that I stopped dreading the times we were home from school."

Involuntarily, Ivy's eyes went to the painting of Merrie and Stuart's father that hung over the fireplace. Stuart resembled Jake York, but the older man had a stubborn jaw and a cruel glimmer in his pale blue eyes.

Like Stuart, he'd been a tall man, lean and muscular. The children had been without a mother, who died giving birth to Merrie. Their mother's sister had stayed with the family and cared for Merrie until she was in grammar school. She and the elder York had argued about his treatment of Stuart, which had ended in her departure. After that, tenderness and unconditional love were things the York kids read about. They learned nothing of them from their taciturn, demanding father. Stuart's defiance only made him more bitter and ruthless.

"But your father built this ranch," Ivy said. "Surely he had to like cattle."

"He did. It was just that football was his whole life," Merrie replied. "You might have noticed that you don't ever see football games here. Stuart cuts off the television at the first mention of it."

"I can see why."

"Dad spent the time between football games running the ranch and his real estate company. He died of a heart attack when I was thirteen, sitting at the boardroom table. He had a violent argument with one of his directors about some proposed expansions that would have placed the company dangerously close to bankruptcy. He was a gambler. Stuart isn't. He always calculates the odds before he makes any decision. He never has arguments with the board of directors." She frowned. "Well, there was one. They insisted that he hire a pilot to fly him to business meetings."

"Why?"

Merrie chuckled. "To stop him from driving himself to them. Didn't I mention that this is his second new XJ in six months?"

Ivy lifted her eyebrows. "What happened to the first one?"

"Slow traffic."

"Come again?"

"He was in a hurry to a called meeting of the board of directors," Merrie said. "There was a little old man driving a motor home about twenty miles an hour up a hill on a blind curve. Stuart tried to pass him. He almost made it, too," she added. "Except that Hayes Carson was coming down the hill on the other side of the road in his squad car."

"What happened?" Ivy prompted when Merrie sat silently.

"Stuart really is a good driver," his sister asserted, "even if he makes insane decisions about where to pass. He spun the car around and stopped it neatly on the shoulder before Hayes got anywhere near him. But Hayes said he could have killed somebody and he wasn't getting out of a ticket. The only way he got his license back was that he promised to go to traffic school and do public service."

"That doesn't sound like your brother."

Merrie shrugged. "He did go to traffic school twice, and then he went to the sheriff's department and showed Hayes Carson how to reorganize his department so that it operated more efficiently."

"Did Hayes actually ask him to do that?"

"No. But Stuart argued that reorganizing the chaos in the sheriff's department *was* a public service. Hayes didn't agree. He went and talked to Judge Meacham himself. They gave Stuart his license back."

"You said he didn't hit anything with the car."

"He didn't. But while it was sitting on the side of the road, a cattle truck—one of his own, in fact—took the curve too fast and sideswiped it off the shoulder down a ten-foot ravine."

"I don't guess the driver works for you anymore," Ivy mused.

"He does, but not as a driver," Merrie said, laughing. "Considering how things could have gone, it was a lucky escape for everyone. It was a sturdy, well-built car, but those cattle trucks are heavy. It was a total loss."

"Even if I could afford a car, I don't think I want to learn how to drive," Ivy commented. "It seems safer not to be on the highway when Stuart's driving."

"It is."

They snacked on cheese and crackers and finger sandwiches and cookies, and sipped coffee in perfect peace for several minutes.

"Ivy, are you sure you're cut out to be a public accountant?" Merrie asked after a minute.

Ivy laughed. "What brought that on?"

"I was just thinking about when we were still in high school," she replied. "You had your heart set on singing opera."

"And chance would be a fine thing, wouldn't it?" Ivy

asked with a patient smile. "The thing is, even if I had the money to study in New York, I don't want to leave Jacobsville. So that sort of limits my options. Singing in the church choir does give me a chance to do what I love most."

Merrie had to agree that this was true. "What you should really do is get married and have kids, and teach them how to sing," she replied with a grin. "You'd be a natural. Little kids flock around you everywhere we go."

"What a lovely idea," she enthused. "Tell you what, you gather up about ten or twelve eligible bachelors, and I'll pick out one I like."

That set Merrie to laughing uproariously. "If we could do it that way, I might get married myself," she confessed. "But I'd have to have a man who wasn't afraid of Stuart. Talk about limited options . . . !"

"Hayes Carson isn't scared of him," Ivy pointed out. "You could marry him."

"Hayes doesn't want to get married. He says he likes his life uncluttered by emotional complications."

"Lily-livered coward," Ivy enunciated. "No guts."

"Oh, he's got guts. He just doesn't think marriage works. His parents fought like tigers. His younger brother, Bobby, couldn't take it, and he turned to drugs and overdosed. It had to affect Hayes, losing his only sibling like that."

"He might fall in love one day."

"So might my brother," Merrie mused, "but if I were a betting woman, I wouldn't bet on that any time soon."

"Love is the great equalizer."

"Love is a chemical reaction," Merrie, the nursing student, said dryly. "It's nothing more than a physical response to a sensory stimulus designed to encourage us to replicate our genes."

"Oh, yuuuck!" Ivy groaned. "Merrie, that's just gross!"

"It's true—ask my anatomy professor," Merrie defended.

"No, thank you. I'll take my own warped view of it as a miracle, thanks."

Merrie laughed, then she frowned. "Ivy, what are you eating?" she asked abruptly.

"This?" She held up a cookie from the huge snack platter that contained crackers, cheese, cakes, little finger sandwiches and cookies. Mrs. Rhodes loved to make hors d'oeuvres. "It's a cookie."

Merrie looked worried. "Ivy, it's a chocolate cookie," came the reply. "You know you'll get a migraine if you eat them."

"It's only one cookie," she defended herself.

"*And* there's a low pressure weather system dumping rain on us, *and* you've had the stress of Rachel worrying you to death since your father's funeral," she replied. "Not to mention that your father's only been dead for a few weeks. There's always more than one trigger that sets off a migraine, even if you don't realize what they are. Stuart gets them, too, you know, but it's red wine or aged cheese that causes his."

Ivy recalled one terrible attack that Stuart had after he'd closed a tricky big business deal. It had been the day after he'd attended a band concert at Ivy and

Merrie's school soon after the girls had become friends. They were both in band. It had been Ivy who'd suggested strong coffee and then a doctor for Stuart. He'd never realized that his terrible sick headaches were, in fact, migraines, much less that there were prescriptions for them that actually worked. Ivy had suffered from them all her life. Her mother and her mother's father had also had migraine headaches. They tended to run in families. They ran in Stuart's, too. Even though Merrie hadn't had one, her father had suffered with them. So had an uncle.

"The doctor gave Stuart the preventative, after diagnosing the headache," Merrie commented.

"I can't take the preventative," Ivy replied. "I have a heart defect, and the medication causes abnormal heart rhythms in me. I have to treat the symptoms instead of the disease."

"I hope you brought your medicine."

Ivy looked at the chocolate cookie and ruefully put the remainder down on her plate. "I forgot to get it refilled." Translated, that meant that she couldn't afford it anymore. There was one remedy that was sold over the counter. She took it in desperation, although it wasn't as effective as the prescription medicines were.

"Stuart has pain medicine as well as the preventative," Merrie said solemnly. "If you wake up in the night screaming in pain because of that cookie, we can handle it. Maybe when your father's estate is settled, Rachel will leave you alone."

Ivy shook her head. "Rachel won't rest until she gets

31

every penny. She convinced Dad that I was wilder than a white-tailed deer. He cut me out of his will."

"He knew better," Merrie said indignantly.

She laughed. "No, he didn't." Nor had he tried to find out. He drank to excess. Rachel encouraged him to do it. When he was drunk, she fed him lies about Ivy. The lies had terrible repercussions. That amused Rachel, who hated her prim younger sister. It made Ivy afraid every day of her life.

She pulled her mind from the past and forced a smile. "If having the estate will keep Rachel in New York, and out of my life, it will be worth it. I still have Aunt Hettie's little dab of money. That, and my part-time job, will see me through school."

"It's so unfair," her friend lamented. "It's never been like that here. Stuart split everything right down the middle between us. He said we were both Dad's kids and one shouldn't be favored over the other."

Ivy frowned. "That sounds as if one was."

She nodded. "In Dad's will, Stuart got seventy-five percent. He couldn't break the will, because Dad was always in his right mind. So he did the split himself, after the will was probated." She smiled. "I know you don't like him, but he's a great brother."

It wasn't dislike. It was fear. Stuart in a temper was frightening to a woman whose whole young life had been spent trying to escape male violence. Well, it was a little more than fear, she had to admit. Stuart made her feel funny when she was around him. He made her nervous.

"He's good to you," Ivy conceded.

"He likes you," she replied. "No, really, he does. He admires the way you work for your education. He was furious when Rachel jerked the house out from under you and left you homeless. He talked to the attorney. It was no use, of course. It takes a lot to break a will."

It was surprising that Stuart would do anything for her. He always seemed to resent her presence in his house. He tolerated her because she was Merrie's best friend, but he was never friendly. In fact, he stayed away from home when he knew Ivy was visiting.

"He's probably afraid of my fatal charm," Ivy murmured absently. "You know, fearful that he might succumb to my wiles." She frowned. "What, exactly, are wiles anyway?"

"If I knew that, I'd probably have a boyfriend," Merrie chuckled. "So it's just as well I don't. I'm going to get my nursing certificate before I get involved with any one man. Meanwhile, I'm playing the field like crazy. There's a resident in our hospital that I adore. He takes me out once in a while, but it's all very low-key." She eyed Ivy curiously. "Any secret suitors in your life?"

Ivy shook her head. "I don't ever want to get married," she said quietly.

Merrie frowned. "Why not?"

"Nobody could live with me," she said. "I snore."

Merrie laughed. "You do not."

"Anyway, I'm like you. I just want to graduate and get a real job." She considered that. "I've dreamed of having my own money, of supporting myself. In a lot of ways, I led a sheltered life. Dad didn't want to lose me, so he discouraged boys from coming around. I was valuable, free hired help. After all, Rachel couldn't cook and she'd never have washed clothes or mopped floors."

Merrie didn't smile. She knew that was the truth. Ivy had been used her whole young life by the people who should have cherished her. She'd never pried, but she noticed that Ivy hardly ever talked about her father, except in a general way.

"You really do keep secrets, don't you?" Merrie asked gently. She held up a hand when Ivy protested. "I won't pry. But if you ever need to talk, I'm right here."

"I know that." She smiled back. "Thanks."

"Now. How about a good movie on the pay channels? I was thinking about that fantasy film everyone's raving about." She named it.

Ivy beamed. "I really wanted to see that one, but it's no fun going to the movies alone."

"I'll ask Mrs. Rhodes for some popcorn to go with it. In fact, she might like to watch it with us. She doesn't have a social life."

"She's married, isn't she?" Ivy probed gently.

"She was," came the reply. "He was an engineer in the Army and he went overseas with his unit. He didn't come back. They had no kids; it was just the two of them for almost twenty years." She grimaced. "She came to us just after it happened, looking for a live-in job. She'd lost everything. He got a good salary and was career Army, so she hadn't worked except as a temporary secretary all that time. When he was gone, she had to go through channels to apply for widow's benefits, and the job market locally was flat. She came to work for us as a temporary thing, and just stayed. We all suited each other."

"She's very sweet."

"She's a nurturing person," Merrie agreed. "She even gets away with nurturing Stuart. Nobody else would dare even try."

Ivy wouldn't have touched that line with a pole. She just nodded.

She was looking through the program guide on the wide-screen television when Merrie came in with a small, plump, smiling woman with short silver hair.

"Hi, Mrs. Rhodes," Ivy said with a smile.

"Good to see you, Ivy. I'm making popcorn. What's the movie?"

"We wanted to see the fantasy one," Merrie explained.

"It's wonderful," came the surprising reply. "Yes, I went to the theater to see it, all by myself," Mrs. Rhodes chuckled. "But I'd love to see it again, if you wouldn't mind the company."

"We'd love it," Ivy said, and meant it.

"Then I'll just run and get the popcorn out of the microwave," the older woman told them.

"I'll buy the movie," Merrie replied, taking the

remote from Ivy. "This is the one mechanical thing I'm really good at—pushing buttons!"

The movie was wonderful, but long before it was over, Ivy was seeing dancing colored lights before her eyes. Soon afterward, she lost the vision in one eye; in the center of it was only a ragged gray static like when a television channel went off the air temporarily. It was the unmistakable aura that came before the sick headaches.

She didn't say a word about it to Merrie. She'd just go to bed and tough it out. She'd done that before. If she could get to sleep before the pain got bad, she could sleep it off most of the time.

She toughed it out until the movie ended, then she yawned and stood up. "Sorry, I've got to get to bed. I'm so sleepy!"

Merrie got up, too. "I could do with an early night myself. Mrs. Rhodes, will you close up?"

"Certainly, dear. Need anything else from the kitchen?"

"Could I have a bottle of water?" Ivy asked. "I always keep one by my bed at home."

"I'll bring it up to you," Mrs. Rhodes promised. "Merrie?"

Merrie shook her head. "No, thanks, I keep diet sodas in my little fridge. I drink enough bottled water at school to float a boat!"

"You said you could lend me a nightgown?" Ivy asked when they were at the top of the staircase.

"Can and will. Come on."

Merrie pulled a beautiful nightgown and robe out of her closet and presented it to Ivy. It was sheer, lacy, palest lemon and absolutely the most beautiful thing Ivy had ever seen. Her nightgowns were cheap cotton ones in whichever colors were on sale. She caught her breath just looking at it.

"It's too expensive," she protested.

"It isn't. It was a gift and I hate it," Merrie said honestly. "You know I never wear yellow. One of my roommates drew my name at Christmas and bought it for me. I didn't have the heart to tell her it wasn't my color, I hugged her and said thank you. Then I hung it in the closet."

"I would have done the same," Ivy had to admit. "Well, it's beautiful."

"It will look beautiful on you. Go on to bed. Sleep late. We won't need to get up before noon if we don't want to."

"I never sleep past seven, even when I try," Ivy said, smiling. "I always got up to make breakfast for Dad and Rachel, and then just for Dad after she left home."

"Mrs. Rhodes will make you breakfast, whenever you want it," Merrie said. "Sleep well."

"You, too."

Ivy went into the bedroom that adjoined Merrie's. There was a bathroom between the guest room and Stuart's room, but Ivy wasn't worried about that. Stuart was out of town and she'd have the bathroom all to herself if she needed it. She probably would, if she couldn't sleep off the headache. They made her violently ill.

She put on the nightgown and looked at herself in the full-length mirror. She was surprised at how she looked in it. Her breasts were small, but high and firm, and the gown emphasized their perfection. It flowed down her narrow waist to her full hips and long, elegant legs. She'd never worn anything so flattering.

With her long blond hair and dark green eyes and silky, soft complexion, she looked like a fairy. She wasn't pretty, but she wasn't plain, either. She was slender and medium height, with a nice mouth and big eyes. Only one of the big eyes was seeing right now, though, and she needed sleep.

There was a soft knock at the door. She opened it, and there was Mrs. Rhodes with the water. "Dear, you're very pale," the older woman said, concerned. "Are you all right?"

Ivy sighed. "It was the chocolate. I've got a headache. I don't want Merrie to know. She worries. I'll just go to sleep, and I'll be fine."

Mrs. Rhodes wasn't convinced. She'd seen Ivy have these headaches, and she'd seen Stuart suffer through them. "Have you got something to take?"

"In my purse," Ivy lied. "I've got aspirin."

"Well, if you need something stronger, you come wake me up, okay?" she asked gently. "Stuart keeps medicine for them. I know where to look."

She smiled. "Thanks, Mrs. Rhodes. I really mean it."

"You just get some sleep. Call if you need me. I'm just across the hall from Merrie."

"I will. Thanks again."

● ● ●

She dropped down on the queen-size bed and pulled the silken covers up over her. The room was a palace compared to her one-room apartment. Even the bathroom was larger than the room she lived in. Merrie took such wealth and luxury for granted, but Ivy didn't. It was fascinating to her.

The pain was vicious. The headaches always settled in one eye, and they felt as if a knife were being pushed right through the pupil. Some people called them "head-bangers" because sufferers had been known to knock their heads against walls in an effort to cope with the pain. Ivy groaned quietly and pushed her fist against the eye that had gone blind. The sight had returned to it, and the pain came with it.

Volumes had been written on the vicious attacks. Comparing them to mild tension headaches was like comparing a hurricane to a spring breeze. Some people lost days of work every year to them. Others didn't realize what sort of headaches they were and never consulted a doctor about them. Still others wound up in emergency rooms pleading for something to ease the pain. Hardly anything sold over the counter would even faze them. It usually took a prescription medicine to make them bearable. Ivy had never found anything that would stop the pain, regardless of its strength. The best she could hope for was that the pain would ease enough that she could endure it until it finally stopped.

Around midnight, the pain spawned nausea and she was violently sick. By that time, the pain was a throbbing, stabbing wave of agony.

She dabbed her mouth and eyes with a wet cloth and laid back down, trying again to sleep. But even though the nausea eased a little, the pain increased.

She would have to go and find Mrs. Rhodes. On the way, she'd stop in the bathroom long enough to wet the cloth again.

She opened the door, half out of her mind with pain, and walked right into a tall, muscular man wearing nothing except a pair of black silk pajama bottoms. Blue eyes bit into her green ones as she looked up, a long way up, into them.

"What the hell are you doing here?" Stuart York demanded with a scowl.

CHAPTER THREE

IVY hadn't seen him in months. They didn't travel in the same circles, and he was never at home when she was visiting Merrie. The sight of him so unexpectedly caused an odd breathlessness, an ache in the pit of her stomach.

He was watching her intently, and there was an odd glint in his pale blue eyes, as if she'd disappointed him. He rarely smiled. He certainly wasn't doing it now. His wide, sexy mouth was thin with impatience. She couldn't take her eyes off him. His chest was broad and muscular and thick with black, curling hair that narrowed on its way down his belly. The silk pajama bottoms clung lovingly to the hard muscles of his thighs.

He was as sexy as any television hero. Even with his thick, straight black hair slightly tousled and his eyes red from lack of sleep, he was every woman's dream.

"I was . . . looking for something," she faltered.

"Me?" he drawled sarcastically, and he reached for her. "Rachel told me all about you before she left town. I didn't believe her at first." His eyes slid down her exquisite body in the revealing gown. "But it looks as though she was right about you all along."

The feel of all that warm strength so close made her legs wobbly. There was the faint scent of soap and cologne that clung to his skin, and the way he was looking at her made it even worse. Over the years, she'd tried very hard not to notice Stuart. But close like this, her heart ran away with her. She felt sensations that made her uneasy, alien sensations that made her want things she didn't understand. She couldn't take her eyes off him, but he was misty in her vision. Her head was throbbing so madly that she couldn't think. Which was unfortunate, because he misinterpreted her lack of protest.

A split second later, she was standing with her back against the cold wall with Stuart's hard body pressing down against hers. His hands propped against the wall, pinning her, while his eyes took in the visible slope of her breasts in the wispy gown. He couldn't seem to stop looking at her.

"I need . . ." she began weakly, trying to focus enough to ask for some aspirin, for anything that might make the headache ease.

". . . me?" he taunted. His voice was deep and velvety soft, husky with emotion as his head bent. His pale eyes went to her parted lips. "Show me, honey."

While she was working out that odd comment, his mouth was suddenly hard and insistent on her own. She stiffened with apprehension. She'd never been so close, so intimately close, to a man before. His mouth was demanding, twisting on hers as though he wanted more than he was getting.

She really should protest the way he was holding her, so that she felt every inch of muscle that pressed against her. But his mouth was erotic, masterful. She'd only been kissed a few times, mostly at parties, and never by a boy who knew much about intimacy. It had been her good fortune that she'd never felt violent attraction to a man who wouldn't accept limits. But her luck had just run out, with Stuart. He knew what he was doing. His mouth eased and became coaxing, caressing. His teeth nipped tenderly at her lower lip, teasing it to move down so that he had access to the whole of her soft, warm mouth.

She shivered a little as passion grew inside her. She felt his bare chest under her hands, and she loved the warmth and strength of him so close. Her fingers burrowed through the thick hair that covered the hard muscle, making them tingle even as she felt the urgent response of his body to the soft caress. She let her lips part as he pressed harder against them and she moved, involuntarily, closer to the source of the sudden pleasure she was feeling.

It was like an invitation, and he took it. His hips ground into hers and she felt the sudden hardness of him against her with real fear. He groaned harshly. His body became even more insistent. He didn't seem capable, at that moment, of stopping.

The throbbing delight she felt turned quickly to fear as his hands dropped to her hips and dragged them against the changing contours of his body with intent enough that even a virgin could feel his rising desire. Frightened by his headlong ardor, she pushed at his chest frantically, trying to drag her lips away from the hard, slow drugging pressure of his mouth.

He was reluctant to stop. He could feel his own body betraying his hunger for her. He couldn't help it. She was exquisite to touch, and she tasted like sweet heaven. He couldn't think past her body under him in the bed behind them. But finally the violence of her resistance got through to his foggy brain. He managed to lift his head just long enough to meet her eyes.

When he saw the fear, he began to doubt for the first time what Rachel had said about her little sister. If this was the permissive behavior that had been described to him, it was unlikely that she'd had many boyfriends. On the contrary, she looked as if she was scared to death of what came next.

"No," she choked huskily, her eyes bright with feeling, pleading with his. "Please don't."

For just an instant, his hands tightened on her waist. But her gasp and stiffening posture told its own story. Promiscuous? This little icicle? Just on the strength of her response, he would have bet his life on her innocence.

As his head began to clear, anger began to smolder in his chest. He'd lost his self-control. He'd betrayed his hunger for her. He couldn't pretend that he hadn't felt desire while he was kissing her. She'd felt his momentary weakness. His own raging desire had betrayed him, with this innocent child-woman who was only eighteen years old. Eighteen!

Anger and shame and guilt overwhelmed him. He pushed her away from him roughly, his eyes blazing as he looked down at her body in the revealing nightgown. Despite everything, he still wanted her, desperately.

"What did you expect, when you go looking for a man, in the middle of the night, dressed like that!?" He emphasized her attire with one big hand.

Shivering, her arms crossed over her breasts. She swayed, putting a hand up to her eye. She'd forgotten the headache for a few seconds while he'd been kissing her, but it came back now with a fury. She leaned back against the wall for support. Stronger than shame, than anger, was pain, stabbing into her right eye like a heated poker.

Her face was white and contorted. It began to occur to him that she was unwell. "What's the matter with you?" he asked belatedly.

"Migraine," she whispered huskily. "I was looking for aspirin."

He made a rough sound in his throat. "Aspirin, for a

migraine," he scoffed. He bent suddenly, swung her up into his arms and strode back into his bedroom with her. The feel of her softness in his arms was intoxicating. She was as light as a feather. He noticed that she wasn't protesting the contact. In fact, her cheek was against his bare chest and he could hear her breathing change, despite the pain he knew she was feeling. "You'll get something stronger than aspirin to stop the pain, but not before I've checked with your doctor. Sit." He put her down on the bed and went to the dresser to pick up his cell phone.

"It's Dr. Lou Coltrain," she began.

He ignored her. He knew who her doctor was. "Lou? Sorry to bother you so late. Ivy Conley's spending the weekend with Merrie, and she's got a migraine. Can she take what you give me for it?"

There was a pause, during which he stared at Ivy, trying not to look at her the way he felt like looking. She was beautifully formed. But her age tortured him. She was too young for him. He was thirty, to her eighteen. He didn't dare touch her again. In order to keep his distance, he was going to have to hurt her. He didn't want to, but she was looking at him in a different way already. The kiss had been very much a shared pleasure until he'd turned up the heat and frightened her.

A minute later he shifted, listened, nodded. "Okay. Yes, I'll send her in to the clinic tomorrow if she isn't better by morning. Thanks."

He hung up. "She said that you can have half the dose I take," he said, pulling a prescription bottle from his top drawer and shaking out one pill. He poured water from a carafe into a crystal glass and handed her the pill and the glass. "Take it. If you're not better in the morning, you'll need to go to her clinic and be seen."

"Could you stop glaring at me?" she asked through the pain.

"You aren't the only one who's got a pain," he said bluntly. "Take it!"

She flushed, but she put the pill in her mouth and swallowed it down with two big sips of water.

He took the glass from her, helped her up from the bed and marched her back through the bathroom to her own room. He guided her down onto the bed.

"I didn't know you'd be home," she defended herself. "Merrie promised you wouldn't. I didn't expect to walk into the bathroom and run into you."

"That goes double for me. I didn't know you were on the place," he added curtly. "My sister has a convenient memory."

In other words, she hadn't told him Ivy was here. Ivy wondered if her friend knew he was due back home. It would have been a dirty trick to play, and Merrie was bigger than that. So maybe she hadn't known.

"Thank you for the pill," she said tautly.

He let out a harsh breath. "You're welcome. Go to bed."

She slid the covers back and eased under them, wincing as the movement bumped the pain up another notch.

"And don't read anything romantic into what just happened," he added bluntly. "Most men are vulnerable at night, when temptation walks in the door scantily clad."

"I didn't know . . . !"

He held up a hand. "All right. I'll take your word for it." His eyes narrowed. "Your sister fed me a pack of lies about you. Why?"

"Why were you even talking to her about me?" she countered. "You always said you couldn't stand her, even when you were in the same class in high school."

"She phoned me when your father died."

"Ah, yes," she said, closing her eyes. "She didn't want to take any chances that you might come down on my side of the fence during the probate of the will." She laughed coldly. "I could have told her that would never happen."

"She thought you might ask Merrie for help."

She opened her eyes. The pain was throbbing. She could see her heartbeat in her own eyes. "She would have. Not me. I can stand on my own two feet."

"Yes," he said slowly, studying her pale face. "You've done remarkably well."

That was high praise, coming from him. She looked up into his lean face and wondered how it would have felt if she hadn't pulled back. Warm color surged into her cheeks.

"Stop that," he muttered. "I won't be an object of desire to some daydreaming teenager."

His tone wasn't hostile. It was more amused than

angry. Her eyebrows arched. "Are you sure?" she asked, returning the banter. "Because I have to have somebody to cut my teeth on. Just think, I could fall into bad company and become a lost sheep, and it would all be your fault, because you wouldn't let me obsess over you."

At first he thought she was being sarcastic. Then he saw the twinkle in those pretty green eyes.

"You're too young to be obsessing over a mature man. Go pick on a boy your own age."

"That's the problem," she pointed out, pushing her hand against her throbbing eye. "Boys my own age are *just* boys."

"All men started out that way."

"I guess so." She groaned. "Could you please hit me in the head with a hammer? Maybe it would take my mind off the pain."

"It takes pills a long time to work, doesn't it?" he asked. He moved to sit beside her on the coverlet. "Want a cold wet cloth?"

"I'd die before I'd ask you to go and get one."

He laughed shortly. But he got up, went into the bathroom and was back a minute later with a damp washcloth. He pressed it over her eyes. "Does it help?"

She held it there and sighed. "Yes. Thank you."

"I have to have heat," he replied conversationally. "I can't bear cold when my head's throbbing."

"I remember."

"Where did you get the chocolate, Ivy?" he asked after a minute.

She grimaced. He really did know too much about her. "There was a cookie this afternoon. I didn't realize it was chocolate until I'd eaten half of it. Merrie warned me."

"I can eat ten chocolate bars and they don't faze me."

"That's because chocolate isn't one of your triggers. But Merrie says you won't drink red wine."

"Wine is no substitute for a good Scotch whiskey. I gave it up years ago."

"Aged cheese probably has the same effect."

He grimaced. "It does. I love Stilton and I can't eat it."

She smiled. "A weakness! I thought you were beyond them."

"You'd be surprised," he replied, and he was looking at her with an expression he was glad she couldn't see.

The door opened suddenly and Merrie stopped, frozen, in the doorway. "Are you having a pajama party?" she asked the occupants of the room.

"Yes, but you're not invited. It's exclusive to migraine sufferers, and you don't have migraines," he added with a faint smile.

She closed the door and came in, to stand by the bed. "I was afraid of this," she told Ivy. "I should have noticed there was chocolate on the tray."

"She's the one who should have noticed," Stuart said harshly.

"Well, talk about intolerance," Ivy muttered from under the washcloth. "I'll bet nobody fusses at you for what you ate when you've got one of these. I'll bet you'd throw them out the window if they did."

"You're welcome to try throwing me out the window," he offered.

"Don't be silly. I'd never be able to lift you."

"Do you need some aspirin, Ivy?" Merrie asked, sending a glare at her brother.

"I've already given her something."

Merrie was outraged. "We're taught that you never give anything to another person without consulting their physician . . . !"

"I'm glad you know procedure, but so do I," Stuart replied. "I phoned Lou before I gave it to her." He glanced toward the clock on the bedside table. "It should be taking effect very soon."

It was. Ivy could hardly keep her eyes open. "I'm very sleepy," she murmured, amazed at the sudden easing of the pain that had been so horrific at first.

"Good. When you wake up, your head will feel normal again," Stuart told her.

"Thanks, Stuart," she said, the words slurring as the powerful medication did its job.

"You're welcome," he replied. "I know a thing or two about migraines."

"And she taught you a thing or two about seeing the doctor for medicine that actually helped them," Merrie couldn't resist saying.

He didn't reply. His eyes were on Ivy's face as she went to sleep. He lifted the washcloth and took it away. Her eyes were closed. Her breathing regulated. He was glad that the cover was up to her chin, so that he didn't have to see that perfect body again and lie awake all night remembering it.

He got up from the bed, gently so as not to awaken her, the washcloth still clutched in his hand.

"That was nice of you, to get her something to take," Merrie said as they left Ivy's room.

He shrugged. "I know how it feels."

"How did you come out in Oklahoma?" she asked.

"Everything's ready for the auction," he replied. "I still can't believe they let me down like that at the Jacobsville sales barn."

"They don't have a history of messing up the different lots of cattle they sell," she said in their defense.

"One mistake that big can be expensive," he reminded her. "In this economic climate, even we have to be careful. Losing the Japanese franchise hurt us."

"It hurt the Harts and the Dunns worse," she replied. "They'd invested a lot in organic beef to send over there. They were sitting in clover when the ban hit."

"But they recovered quickly, and so did we, by opening up domestic markets for our organic beef. This organic route is very profitable, and it's going to be even more profitable when people realize how much it contributes to good health."

"Our signature brand sells out quickly enough in local markets," she agreed.

"And even better in big city markets," he replied. "How's school?"

She grinned. "I'm passing everything. In two years, I'll be working in a ward."

"You could come home and go to morning coffees and do volunteer work," he reminded her with a smile.

She shook her head, returning the smile. "I'm not cut out for an easy, cushy life. Neither are you. We come from hardworking stock."

"We do." He bent and brushed his mouth over her cheek. "Sleep tight."

"Are you home for the weekend?"

He glanced at her. "Are you wearing body armor?"

"You and Ivy could get along for two days," she pointed out.

"Only if you blindfold me and gag her."

She blinked. "Excuse me?"

"It's an in-joke," he said. "I have to fly to Denver tomorrow to give a speech at the agriculture seminar on the subject of genetically engineered grain," he added.

She grimaced. "Don't come home with a bloody nose this time, will you?"

He shrugged. "I'm only playing devil's advocate," he told her. "We can't make it too easy on people who want to combine animal cells and vegetable cells and call it progress." His pale eyes began to glitter. "One day, down the road, we'll pay for this noble meddling."

She reached up and touched his face. "Okay, go slug it out with the progressives, if you must. I'll treat Ivy to the new *Imax* movie about Mars."

"Mars?"

"She loves Mars," Merrie told him.

"I'd love to send her there," he replied thoughtfully. "We could strap her to a rocket . . ."

"Stop that. She's my best friend."

He shook his head. "The things I do for you," he protested. "Okay, I'll settle for sending her to the moon."

"She's only just lost her father, her house and she'll soon lose her inheritance as well," she said solemnly. "I could strangle Rachel for what she's done."

He could have strangled Rachel himself, for the lies she'd fed him about Ivy. He should have known better. She'd never been forward with men, to his knowledge. He was certain now that she wasn't. But he wondered why Rachel would make a point of downgrading her to him. Perhaps it was as Ivy said—her sister wanted him to stay out of the probate of her father's will. Poor Ivy. She'd never get a penny if Rachel had her way.

"You look very somber," Merrie observed.

"Ivy should have had the house, at least," he said, betraying the line of his thoughts.

"She couldn't have lived there, even if she'd inherited it," she told him. "There's no money for utilities or upkeep. She can barely keep herself in school and pay her rent."

His eyes narrowed. "We could pay it for her."

"I tried," Merrie replied. "Ivy's proud. She won't accept what she thinks of as charity."

"So she works nights and weekends to supplement that pitiful amount of money her aunt left her," he grumbled. "At least one of those mechanics she keeps books for is married and loves to run around with young women."

"He did ask Ivy out," Merrie replied.

He looked even angrier. "And?"

"She accidentally dropped a hammer on his foot," Merrie chuckled. "He limped for a week, but he never asked Ivy out again. The other men had a lot of fun at his expense."

He felt a reluctant admiration for their houseguest. If she'd been older, his interest might have taken a different form. But he had to remember her age.

"Rachel called her today harping about the probate," she said slowly. "I expect that's why she had the migraine. Rachel worries her to death."

"She needs to learn to stand up to her sister."

"Ivy isn't like that. She loves Rachel, in spite of the way she's been treated by her. She doesn't have any other relatives left. It must be lonely for her."

"She'll toughen up. She'll have to." He stretched. "I'm going to bed. I probably won't see you before I leave. I'll be back sometime Monday. You can reach me on my cell phone if anything important comes up."

"Chayce handles the ranch very well. I expect we'll cope," she said, smiling. "Have fun."

"In between fistfights, I might," he teased. "See you."

"See you."

He went back to his room and closed the door. He had to put Ivy out of his mind and never let history repeat itself. Maybe it wouldn't hurt to have himself photographed with some pretty socialite. He didn't like publicity, but he couldn't take the chance that Ivy might warm up to him.

He recalled reluctantly the dossier a private detective had assembled on Ivy's father. The man had been a closet alcoholic and abusive to his late wife as well as Ivy, although he'd never touched Rachel. He'd wanted to know why Ivy had backed away from him once when he'd been yelling at one of the cowboys. He was never going to tell her what he'd learned. But he was careful not to yell when she was nearby. Still, he told himself, he had to discourage her from seeing him as her future. It would be a kindness to kill this attraction before it had a chance to bloom. She was years too young for him.

The rest of the weekend passed without incident. The two women worked on Merrie's anatomy exam. They watched movies and shared their dreams of the future. On Monday morning, Merrie dropped Ivy off at the local college on her way to San Antonio.

"I'll phone you the next time I have a free weekend," Merrie promised as they parted. "Don't let Rachel make you crazy, okay?"

"I'll try," Ivy said, smiling. "It was a lovely weekend. Thanks."

"I had fun, too. We'll do it again. See you!"

"See you!"

Ivy spent the week daydreaming about what had happened in the guest room at Merrie's house. The more she relived the torrid interlude with Stuart, the more she realized how big a part of her life he was. Over the years she'd been friends with Merrie, Stuart had always been close, but in the background. Because of the age difference, he didn't really hang out in the places that Merrie and Ivy frequented. He was already a mature man while they were getting through high school.

But now, with those hard, insistent kisses, everything between them had changed. Ivy had dreams about him now; embarrassing, feverishly hot dreams of a future that refused to go away. Surely he had to feel something for her, even if it was only desire. He'd wanted her. And she'd wanted him just as much. It was a milestone in her young life.

But toward the end of the week, as she waited in line at the grocery store to pay for her meager purchases, she happened to look at one of the more lurid tabloids. And there was Stuart, with a beautiful, poised young woman plastered against his side, looking up at him adoringly. The caption read, Millionaire Texas Cattleman Donates Land to Historical Trust. Apparently the woman in the photo was the daughter of a prominent businessman who was head of the trust in question. She was a graduate of an equally prominent college back east. The article went on to say that there was talk of a merger between the millionaire and the socialite, but both said the rumors were premature.

Ivy's heart shattered like ice. Apparently Stuart hadn't been as overwhelmed by her as she had been by him, and he was making it known publicly. She had no illusions that the story was an accident. Stuart knew people in every walk of life, and he numbered publishers among his circle of friends. He wanted Ivy to know that he hadn't taken her seriously. He'd chosen a public and humiliating way to do it, to make sure she got the point. And she did.

Merrie called her to ask if she'd seen the story.

"Oh, yes," Ivy replied, her tone subdued.

"I don't understand why he'd let himself be used like that," Merrie muttered irritably. It was obvious that she knew nothing of what had happened between her brother and her best friend, or she'd have said so. She never pulled her punches.

"Even the most reclusive person can fall victim to a determined reporter," Ivy said in his defense. "Maybe the photographer caught him at a weak moment."

"Maybe he's giving a public cold shoulder to some woman who's pursuing him, too," Merrie said innocently. "It would be like him. But there hasn't been anybody in his life lately. Nobody regular, I mean. I'm sure he takes women out. He just doesn't get serious about any of them."

"How did you do on your exam?" Ivy asked, deliberately changing the subject.

"Actually, I passed with flying colors, thanks to you."

"You're welcome," came the pert reply. "You can do the same for me when I have my finals."

"That won't be for a while yet. Coming over next weekend?"

Ivy thought quickly. "Merrie, I promised my roommate that I'd drive up to Dallas with her to see her mother. She doesn't like to make that drive alone." It wasn't the whole truth. Lita had asked her to go, and Ivy had promised to think about it. Now, she was sure that she'd agree.

"Well, it's nice of you to do it." There was a pause. "I'm not going to be able to come home much, once I take the job I've been offered at the hospital here. I'll be working twelve-hour shifts four days a week, and a lot of them will be on weekends."

"I understand," Ivy said quickly, thankful that she wouldn't have to come up with so many excuses to escape seeing Stuart again. "When I graduate, I'll be doing some weekend work myself, I'm sure. But when I can afford a car, I can drive up to see you and we can go to a movie or out to eat or something."

"Of course we can." There was a pause. "Ivy, is anything wrong?"

"No," she said at once. "The lawyer is ready to hand over Dad's estate to Rachel. I'm to get a small lump sum. Maybe Rachel will leave me alone now."

"I hope so. Please keep in touch," Merrie added.

"I will," Ivy agreed. But she crossed her fingers. It was suddenly imperative that she find a way to avoid Stuart from now on. She couldn't afford to let her heart settle on him again, especially now that he'd made his own feelings brutally clear. She'd miss Merrie, but the risk was too great. Broken hearts, she assured herself, were best avoided.

CHAPTER FOUR

Two years later . . .

"IVY, would you like a cup of coffee while you work?" her latest client asked from the doorway of the office where she was writing checks and balancing bank statements.

She looked up from her work, smiling, her long blond hair neatly pinned on top of her head. Her green eyes twinkled. "I'd love one, if it isn't too much trouble," she said.

Marcella smiled back. "I just made a pot. I'll bring it in."

"Thanks."

"It's no trouble at all, really. You've saved me from bankruptcy!"

"Not really. I just discovered that you had more money than you thought you did," she replied.

The older woman chuckled. "You say it your way, I'll say it mine. I'll bring the coffee."

Ivy contemplated the nice office she was using and the amazing progress she'd made in the past two years since her disastrous weekend at Merrie's house. She'd been able to give up the part-time job at the garage when Dorie Hart offered her a bookkeeping service, complete with clients. Dorie had enjoyed the work very much, and she'd kept handling the books for her clients long after her marriage to Corrigan Hart. But her growing family kept her too busy to continue with it. Ivy had been a gift from heaven, Dorie told her laughingly. Now she could leave her clients in good hands and retire with a clear conscience.

Dorie had some wonderful accounts. There was a boutique owner, a budding architect, the owner of a custom beef retail shop, an exercise gym and about a dozen other small businesses in Jacobsville. Ivy had met the businesspeople while she was in her last semester of college, when Dorie had approached her with the proposal. Dorie and Lita, who carpooled with Ivy, were friends. Lita had mentioned Ivy's goals and Dorie had gone to see her at the boardinghouse. It had been an incredible stroke of good luck. Ivy had resigned herself to working in a C.P.A. firm. Now she was a businesswoman in her own right.

And as if her blessings hadn't multiplied enough, she'd also volunteered to do the occasional article for the Jacobs County Cattlemen's Association in what little free time she had. She would have done it as a favor to the Harts, since Corrigan was this year's president, but they wouldn't hear of it. She got a check for anything she produced. Like her math skills, her English skills were very good.

Merrie was nursing at a big hospital in San Antonio. The two spoke on the phone at least twice a month, but they stayed too busy for socializing. Ivy had never told her friend what had happened that last night she spent under Stuart's roof. She never asked about Stuart, either. Merrie seemed to sense that something had gone wrong, but she didn't pry. She didn't talk about her brother, either.

Autumn turned the leaves on the poplars and maples beautiful shades of gold and scarlet. Ivy felt restless, as if something was about to change in her life. She did her job and tried not to think about Stuart York, but always in the back of her mind was the fear of something unseen and unheard. A premonition.

There was a party to benefit a local animal shelter, which Shelby Jacobs had organized. Ivy wouldn't have gone, but Sheriff Hayes Carson was on the committee that had planned the party, and he was showing an increasing interest in Ivy.

She didn't know if she liked it or not. She was fond of Hayes, but her heart didn't do cartwheels when he was around. Maybe that was a good thing.

When he showed up at her boardinghouse late one Friday afternoon, she sat on the porch swing with him. Her room contained little more than a bed and a vanity, and she was uncomfortable taking a man there. Hayes seemed to know that, because he sat down in the swing with no hesitation at all.

"We're having the benefit dance next Friday night," he told her. "Go with me."

She laughed nervously. "Hayes, I haven't danced in years. I'm not sure I even remember how."

His dark eyes twinkled. "I'll teach you."

She studied him with pursed lips. He really was a dish. He had thick blond hair that the sun had streaked, and a lean, serious face. His dark eyes were deep-set, heavy browed. His uniform emphasized his muscular physique. He was built like a rodeo rider, tall, with wide shoulders, narrow hips and long, powerful legs. Plenty of single women around Jacobsville had tried to land him. None had succeeded. He was the consummate bachelor. He seemed immune to women. Most of the time, he looked as if he had no sense of humor at all. He rarely smiled. But he could be charming when he wanted to, and he was turning on the charm now.

Ivy hadn't been asked out in months, and the man who'd asked had a reputation that even Merrie knew about, and Merrie didn't live at home anymore.

Having turned down the potential risk, Ivy kept to herself. Now Hayes was asking her to a dance. She walked around in jeans. She looked and acted like a tomboy. She frowned.

"Come on," he coaxed. "All work and no play will run you crazy."

"You ought to know," she tossed back. "Didn't you take your last vacation day four years ago?"

He chuckled deeply. "I gucss so. I love my job."

"We all noticed," she said. "Between you and Cash Grier, drug dealers have left trails of fire behind them running for the border."

"We've got a good conviction rate," he had to admit. "What's holding you back? Nursing a secret passion for someone hereabouts?"

She laughed. It was half true, but she wasn't admitting it. "Not really," she said. "But I'm not used to socializing. I didn't even do it in college."

He frowned. "I know why you don't date, Ivy," he said unexpectedly. "You can't live in the past. And not every man is like your father."

Her face closed up. Her hands clenched in her lap. She stared out at the horizon, trying not to let the memories eat at her consciousness. "My mother used to say that she thought he was a perfect gentleman before they married. They went together for a year before she married him. And then she discovered how brutal a man he really was. She was pregnant, and she had no place to go."

He caught one of her small hands in his big one. "He was an outsider," he reminded her. "He moved here from Nevada. Nobody knew much about him. But you know people in Jacobsville." He pursed his lips. "I daresay you know all about me."

That droll tone surprised her into laughing. "Well, yes, I do. Everybody does. The only brutal thing about you is your temper, and you don't hit people unless they hit you first."

"That's right. So you'd be perfectly safe with me for one evening."

She sighed. "You're hard to refuse."

"You'll have fun. So will I. Come on," he coaxed. "We'll help add some kennel space to the animal shelter and give people something to gossip about."

"It would be fun," she came back. "You don't date anybody locally."

He shrugged. "I like my own company too much. Besides," he said ruefully, "there's Andy. He stunts my social life."

She shivered. "I'm not going home with you," she pointed out.

"I know. I haven't found a single woman who will." He sighed resignedly. "He's really very tame. He's a vegetarian. He won't even eat a mouse."

"It won't work. Your scaly roommate is going to keep you single, just like Cag Hart's did."

"I've had him for six years," he said. "He's my only pet."

"Good thing. He'd eat any other pet you brought home."

He scowled. "He's a vegetarian."

"Are you sure? Have any dogs or cats disappeared on your place since you got him?" she teased.

He made a face at her. "It's silly to be afraid of a vegetarian. It's like being afraid of a cow!"

Her eyebrows arched. "Andy doesn't look like any cow I ever saw," she retorted. "His picture was on the front page of the paper when you took him to that third grade class to teach them about herpetology. I believe there was some talk about barring you from classrooms . . . ?"

He glowered. "He wasn't trying to attack that girl. She was the tallest kid in the room, and he tried to climb her, that's all."

She had to fight laughter. "I'll bet you won't take him out of the cage at a grammar school ever again," she said.

"You can bet on that," he agreed. He frowned thoughtfully. "I expect he'll have a terror of little girls for the rest of his life, poor old thing."

She shook her head. "Well, I'm not going into the room with him unless he's confined."

"He hates cages. He's too big for most of them, anyway. Besides, he sits on top of the fridge and eats bugs."

"You need to get out more," she pointed out.

"I'm trying to, if you'll just agree," he shot back.

She sighed. "All right, I'll go. But people will gossip about us for weeks."

"I don't care. I'm immune to gossip. So are you," he added when she started to protest.

"I guess I am. Okay. I'll go. Is it jeans and boots?"

"No," he replied. "It's nice dresses and high heels."

"I hate dressing up," she muttered.

"So do I. But I can stand it if you can. And it's for a good cause," he added.

"Yes, it is."

"So, I'll pick you up here at six next Friday night."

She smiled. "I'll buy a dress."

"That's the spirit!"

Word got around town that she was going to the dance with Hayes. Nobody ever knew exactly how gossip traveled so fast, but it was as predictable as traffic flow in rush hour.

Even Merrie heard about it, although Ivy had no idea how. She phoned her best friend two days before the dance.

"Hayes actually asked you out?" Merrie exclaimed.

"But he doesn't date anybody! At least, he hasn't dated anybody since that Jones girl who dumped him for the visiting Aussie millionaire."

"That was two years ago," Ivy agreed, "and I still don't think he's really over her. We're only going to a dance, Merrie. He hasn't asked me to marry him."

"You never know, though, do you?" the other girl wondered aloud. "He might be feeling lonely. He loves kids."

"Slow down!" Ivy exclaimed. "I don't want to get married any more than Hayes does!"

"Why not?"

"I like living by myself," she said evasively. "Anyway, I expect Hayes doesn't know that many single women."

"There are plenty of divorced ones around," came the droll reply.

"The dance will benefit our animal shelter," Ivy told her. "It will add new kennels. We've got so many strays. It's just pitiful."

"I like animals, too, but Hayes isn't asking you to any dance because of stray dogs, you mark my word. Maybe he's going to flash you to deter some woman who's chasing him. That's the sort of thing my brother does."

"Your brother is better at it than Hayes is," Ivy said, not wanting to think of Stuart. She hadn't seen him in a long time.

"Well, of course he is. He gets plenty of practice." There was a sigh. "Except he doesn't seem to be dating anybody lately. I asked him why and he said it wasn't fun anymore. If I didn't know him better, I'd think he'd found someone he wanted to get serious about."

"That's unlikely," Ivy said, but she wondered if Merrie was right. It made her sad.

"Unlikely, but not impossible. I think I might come to the dance, too," she said out of the blue. "I can get someone to work my shift. Everybody owes me favors."

"Who will you come with?"

"I'll come by myself," Merrie returned. "I don't need a date. Tell Hayes to save me a dance, though."

Ivy laughed. "He can take both of us. That will really shake people up locally. They'll think he's putting around a new sort of double-dating."

Merrie laughed, too. "I had a flaming crush on Hayes when we were in high school, but he couldn't see me for dust. That was about the time he fell in with the she-tiger who ditched him for the Aussie. Served him right. Anybody could see that she was only a gold digger."

"Hayes owns his own ranch," she began.

"And he inherited a trust from his grandfather," Merrie agreed. "But Hayes isn't the sort to live on an income he didn't earn. He's like Stuart. They're both independent."

"Same as you," Ivy accused.

She laughed. "I guess so."

"How do you like being a nurse?"

"I love it," Merrie said honestly. "I've never enjoyed

anything so much. I love knowing that I helped keep someone alive. It's the best job in the whole world."

"Merrie, you work all day with sick people," Ivy pointed out.

"Sick people? Me? Are you sure?"

"You work in a hospital," Ivy returned.

"No kidding? No wonder there are sick people everywhere!"

Ivy laughed. "Okay, you made your point. You're in the right place. I'm glad you like your job. You might not believe it, but I like mine just as much. I'm working with some really interesting people."

"So I've heard," Merrie replied. "I'm glad you're happy. But speaking of pleasant things, have you heard from Rachel?"

Ivy's happy face fell. She drew in a long breath. "As a matter of fact, I haven't. Not in over two months. The last I heard, she was trying to get away from Jerry the drug dealer so that she could shack up with a richer man. She wouldn't tell me his name. She did mention that he was married."

"Married. Why doesn't that surprise me?"

"I could barely make sense of what she said," Ivy replied. "She slurred her words so badly that she was incoherent. I can't imagine what a rich man would see in a woman who stays stoned all the time. How she can still act in that condition is beyond me."

"As long as she's leaving you alone, that has to be a bonus."

"I suppose. I just worry about her. She's the only

living relative I have," she added. "Maybe the rich guy will wean her off drugs and get her away from Jerry for good. Unless his wife finds out." She groaned. "That's just what it would take to send Rachel over the edge. I'm sure she's convinced herself that he'll divorce his wife to stay with her. I don't think he will."

"Most of them don't," Merrie agreed. "Did she argue with the drug dealer?"

"I have no idea. But from what I understood, she thinks she's landed in a field of clover. The rich guy buys her diamonds."

"I won't ask what he gets in return."

Ivy grimaced. "Neither would I."

"Well, I'll see you at the dance. Where is it, and when?"

Ivy gave her the particulars, but she was morose when she hung up. What if Rachel was involved with someone well-known and the wife found out and went after her in the press? Rachel was brassy and demanding and totally lacking in compassion. But she was weak in every other way. A scandal would drive her over the edge. There was no telling what she might do.

There had been something unusual in their last conversation as well. Rachel had asked her to pass a message along to the owner of the only bakery in town, the Bun Shop. It hadn't made sense to Ivy; something about a shipment of flour that hadn't arrived on schedule. She wanted to know why Rachel was concerned with a bake shop. Rachel said it was a friend who needed the message passed along.

That conversation had been more volatile than she felt comfortable divulging to Merrie. Rachel had mentioned the ultimatum she'd given her rich lover, that either he divorce his wife or she'd go public with the truth of their relationship. Ivy had pleaded with her to do no such thing, that if the man was that rich, his wife could hire someone to hurt her. Rachel had only laughed, saying that the wife was a cold fish who was half out of her mind, and that she posed no threat at all. But in case that fell through, she said, she'd discovered another good way to get a lot of money. She taunted Ivy with her newfound sources of wealth, intimating that Ivy couldn't get a man even if she had millions. Ivy didn't care. She was tired of Rachel's sarcasm.

They'd parted on not good terms. Rachel had accused her of being jealous. She'd never gotten the attention Rachel had, not even from their father. Ivy was just a loser, Rachel said, and she'd never be more than a clerk. Ivy had agreed that Rachel had gotten more attention at home, by lying about Ivy to their father and letting her take the punishment their father had deemed appropriate for her supposed sins.

Rachel had sounded shocked at the description of their father's idea of punishment. Ivy was lying, she'd accused. The old man hadn't had a violent bone in his body. He loved Rachel, Ivy reminded her sister bitterly. Ivy was just the servant, and the more Rachel denounced her, the more critical and angry he became.

For a few seconds, Rachel actually sounded

regretful. But it passed, as those rare bouts of sympathy always did. Rachel hung up abruptly, mumbling that her lover was at the door.

Ivy put down the phone and realized that she was shaking. Reliving those last days Rachel was at home made her miserable. Her memories were terrible.

She did go shopping for a dress, but the boutique owner she kept books for insisted on letting her borrow one of her own designs for the affair.

"It's my display model," Marcella Black insisted, "and just your size. Besides, it's the exact shade of green that your eyes are. You come by here at five, and I'll help you into it and I'll do your hair and makeup as well. No arguments. You're going to be a fairy princess Friday night."

"I'll turn into the frog at midnight," Ivy teased.

"Fat chance."

"All right. I'll come by at five on Friday. And thanks, Marcella. Really."

The older woman wrinkled her nose affectionately. "You just tell everybody who made that dress for you, and we're even."

"You bet I will!"

Hayes wasn't wearing his uniform. He had on a dark suit with a white cotton shirt and a blue patterned tie. His shoes were so shiny that they reflected the porch light at Mrs. Brown's rooming house.

Ivy had just returned in the little used VW she'd

bought and learned to drive two years earlier from Marcella's boutique, where she'd been dressed and her long blond hair had been put up in a curly coiffure. She had on just enough makeup to make her look sensational. She was shocked at the results. She'd never really tried to look good. Her mirror told her that she did.

Hayes gave her a long, appreciative stare. "You look lovely," he said quietly. He produced a plastic container with a cymbidium orchid inside. He offered it with a little shrug. "She said that women wear them on their wrists these days."

"Yes," she said, "so they don't get crushed when we dance. You didn't have to do this, Hayes," she said, taking the orchid out of the box. "But thank you. It's just beautiful."

"I thought you might like it. Ready to go?"

She nodded, pulling the door closed behind her. She had a small evening bag that Marcella had loaned her to go with the dress. She really did feel like Cinderella.

The community center was full to the brim with local citizens supporting the animal shelter. Two of the veterinarians who volunteered at the animal clinic were there with their spouses, and most of the leading lights of Jacobsville turned up as well. Justin and Shelby Ballenger came with their three sons. The eldest was working at the feedlot with Justin during the summer and working on his graduate degree in animal husbandry the rest of the year. The other two boys were still in high school, but ready to graduate. The three of them looked like their father, although the youngest had Shelby's blue-gray eyes. The Tremayne brothers and the Hart boys came with their wives. Micah Steele and his Callie came, and so did the Doctors Coltrain, Lou and her husband "Copper." J. D. Langley and Fay, and Matt Caldwell and his wife Leslie, and Cash Grier with his Tippy were also milling around in the crowd. Ivy spotted Judd Dunn and his wife, Christabel, in a corner, looking as much in love as when they'd first married.

"Amazing, isn't it, that the hall could hold all these people?" Hayes remarked as he led Ivy up the steps into the huge log structure.

"It really is. I'll bet they'll be able to add a whole new kennel with what they make tonight."

He smiled down at her. "I wouldn't doubt it."

They bumped into another couple, one of whom was Willie Carr, who owned the bakery. Then she remembered Rachel's odd message that she was supposed to give him.

"Willie, Rachel asked me to tell you something," she said, frowning as she struggled to remember exactly what it was.

Willie, tall and dark, looked uncomfortable. He laughed. "Now why would Rachel be sending me messages?" he asked, glancing at his wife. "I'm not cheating on you, baby, honest!"

"Oh, no, it wasn't that sort of message," Ivy said quickly. "It was something about a shipment of flour you were expecting that didn't arrive."

Willie cleared his throat. "I don't know anything about any shipment of flour that would go to New York City, Ivy," he assured her. "Rachel must have been talking about somebody else."

"Yes, I guess she must have. Sorry," she said with a sheepish smile. "She's incoherent most of the time lately."

"I'd say she is, if she's sending me messages about flour!" Willie agreed. He nodded at her and then at Hayes, and drew his wife back out onto the dance floor.

Hayes caught her hand and pulled her aside. "What shipment of flour was Rachel talking about?" he asked suddenly, and he wasn't smiling.

"I really don't know. She just said to tell Willie one was missing. She doesn't even eat sweets . . ."

"How long ago did she tell you to give Willie that message?" he persisted.

"About two days ago," she said. She frowned. "Why?"

Hayes took her by the hand and drew her along the dance floor to where Cash Grier was standing at the punch bowl with his gorgeous redheaded wife, Tippy.

"How's it going?" Cash greeted them, shaking hands with Hayes.

Hayes stepped closer. "Rachel sent Willie over there—" he jerked his head toward Willie, who was oblivious to the attention he was getting "—a message."

Cash was all business at once. "What message?"

Hayes prompted Ivy to repeat it.

"Code?" Cash asked Hayes.

The other man nodded. "It was two days ago that Ivy got the message."

Cash's dark eyes twinkled. "What a coincidence."

"Yes."

"Which proves that connection we were discussing earlier." He turned to Ivy. "If your sister sends any more messages to Willie, or anyone else, by you, tell Hayes, would you?"

She was all at sea. "Rachel's mixed up in something, isn't she?"

"Not necessarily," Hayes said at once. "But she knows someone who is, we think. Don't advertise this, either."

Ivy shook her head. "I'm no gossip." She grimaced. "Rachel's getting mixed up with some rich man, and she's trying to get away from her boyfriend, who deals drugs. The rich man is married. I'm afraid it's all going to end badly."

"People who get involved with drugs usually do end badly," Hayes said somberly.

"Yes, they do," Ivy had to agree. She smiled at Tippy, who was wearing a green and white dress made of silk and chiffon. "You look lovely."

"Thanks," Tippy replied, smiling. "So do you, Ivy. Marcella made my dress, you know. She made yours, too, didn't she?"

Ivy nodded, grinning. "She's amazing."

"I think so, too," Tippy agreed. "I've sent photos of her work to some friends of mine in New York. Don't tell her. It's a surprise."

"If anything comes of it, she'll be so thrilled. That was sweet of you."

Tippy waved away the compliment. "She's so talented, she deserves a break."

"Well, I came here to dance," Hayes informed them, taking Ivy's hand.

Cash pursed his lips. "Really?"

"I know I'm not in your league, Grier," Hayes said dourly, "but I can do the Macarena, if we can get somebody to play it."

"You can?" Cash chuckled. "By a strange coincidence, so can I. And I taught her." He indicated Tippy.

"In that case," Hayes replied, grinning, "may the best sheriff win."

And he went off to talk to the bandleader.

The band stopped suddenly, talked among the members and they all started grinning when Hayes came back to wrap his arm around Ivy.

"One, two, three, *four,*" the bandleader counted off, and the band broke into the Macarena.

Ivy knew the steps, having watched a number of important people dance it on television some years before. She wasn't the only one who remembered. The dance floor filled up with laughing people.

Hayes performed the quick hand motions with expertise, laughing as hard as Ivy was. They got through the second chorus and Ivy almost collapsed into Hayes's strong arms, resting her cheek against his chest.

"I'm out of shape!" she exclaimed breathlessly. "I need to get out more!"

"Just what I was thinking," he replied, smiling down at her.

Ivy happened to glance toward the doorway at that moment. Her gaze met a pair of pale blue eyes that were glittering like a diamondback rattlesnake coiling. Ivy's heart ran away as Stuart York gave her a look that could have fried bread.

CHAPTER FIVE

Ivy had never seen that particular expression in Stuart's pale eyes, and she was amazed that he seemed so furious. Beside him, Merrie was also watching her with Hayes, and even though she smiled, she seemed a little shocked.

The two Yorks moved through the crowd, pausing now and again to exchange greetings as they came to stand beside Ivy and Hayes, who had broken apart by then. Ivy stared helplessly at Stuart. It had been a long time since she'd seen him. She knew that he'd been avoiding her ever since the unexpected and explosive interlude that last night she'd spent at Merrie's house, over two years ago.

If she was self-conscious, he wasn't. His pale eyes were narrow, glittering, dangerous as they met hers.

"I thought you didn't dance, Hayes," Merrie said. She was smiling, but she seemed ill at ease.

"I don't, as a rule," he agreed, smiling back. "But I can manage it once in a while."

"We're all here to support the local animal shelter," Ivy told Merrie. "From the looks of this crowd, they're going to end up with plenty of donations."

"I send them a check every year," Stuart said curtly.

"Did you two come together?" Hayes asked curiously.

"We were both at a loose end tonight," Merrie replied. "I got someone to cover for me at the hospital. I really came because I knew Ivy would be here. I haven't seen her in so long!"

Ivy was bemused. She wondered why Merrie seemed so unlike herself.

"I never believed you'd make a nurse," Hayes told Merrie with a grin. "I still remember you fainting when we had to sew up a wound on that old horse you used to trot around on."

"I wish I could forget." Merrie groaned. "It wouldn't have been so bad, except for where I landed."

"It was the only fresh manure on the place," Stuart inserted with a chuckle. "I swear she took three baths that day before she got rid of the smell."

The band started up again, this time playing a dreamy slow tune. Hayes looked down at Merrie. "Want to dance?"

She hesitated.

"Go on," Ivy coaxed, smiling.

Merrie relaxed a little and let Hayes take her hand. He led her onto the dance floor and into a lazy box step. Was it Ivy's imagination, or did Merrie look as if she'd landed in paradise, wrapped up in Hayes Carson's strong arms?

"Do you dance, Mr. York?" Tippy asked.

He shook his head, sliding his big hands into his pockets. "Afraid not."

She smiled. "Neither do I. At least, not very well. I'm learning, though."

Cash drew her to his side. "Yes, you are, baby," he said affectionately. "Come on. We can always do with a little practice. See you both later," he added.

Which left Ivy alone with Stuart for the first time in over two years. She was ill at ease and it showed.

He turned and looked down at her deliberately, his pale eyes narrow and searching. "I like the dress," he said, his voice deep and slow.

"Thanks," she said, a little self-conscious because of the way he was looking at her. "I keep books for a boutique owner. It's a model she's hoping to sell."

"So what are you, walking advertising?" he asked.

She smiled. "I suppose so."

He glanced at his sister dancing with Hayes. "She used to have a horrific crush on him," he said out of the blue. "I was glad when she outgrew it. Hayes takes chances. He's been in two serious gun battles since he became sheriff. He barely walked away from the last one. She'd never make a lawman's wife."

"She made a nurse," she pointed out.

"Yes, well, patients go home when they've healed. But a lawman's wife waits up all hours, hoping he'll come home at all." He looked down at her. "There's a difference."

She felt guilty when she remembered the way Merrie had looked when Hayes asked her to dance, as if she'd trespassed on someone else's property. Considering Stuart's attitude, it wasn't out of the realm of possibility that Merrie might be hiding her interest in Hayes. Stuart liked him, but he'd always said that Hayes was too old for his sister, not to mention being in one of the more dangerous professions. Merrie idolized her brother. She wouldn't deliberately cross him.

"Why are you here with Hayes?" he asked abruptly.

She blinked at the boldness of the question. She should have told him it was none of his business. But she couldn't. He had that air of authority that had always opened doors for him.

"He didn't want to come alone and neither did I," she said.

"He's well off, and he's a bachelor," he replied.

"Are you making a point?" she asked.

His eyes narrowed on her face. "You'll be twenty-one soon."

She was surprised that he kept up with her age. "Yes, I suppose so."

He didn't blink. "Merrie said you wanted to study opera."

"Then she must have also said that I don't want to leave Jacobsville," she replied. "It would be a waste of time to train for a career I don't want."

"Do you want to keep books for other people for the rest of your life?"

"I like keeping books. You might remember that I also do the occasional article for the local cattlemen's association."

He didn't reply to that. His eyes went back to his sister, moving lazily around the dance floor with Hayes. After a minute, his big hand reached down and caught Ivy's. He tugged her gently onto the dance floor and slid his hand around her waist.

"You said you didn't dance," she murmured breathlessly.

He shrugged. "I lied." He curled her into his body and moved gracefully to the music, coaxing her cheek onto his chest. His arm tightened around her, bringing her even closer.

She could barely breathe. The proximity was intoxicating. It brought back that one sweet interlude between them, so long ago. It was probably a dream and she'd wake up clutching a pillow in her own bed. So why not enjoy it, she thought? She closed her eyes, gave him her weight, and sighed. For an instant, she could almost have sworn that a shudder passed through his tall body.

She felt his lips against her forehead. It was the closest to heaven she'd ever come.

But all too soon it was over. The music ended and Stuart stepped away from her.

She felt cold and empty. She wrapped her arms around herself and forced a smile that she didn't really feel.

Stuart was watching her intently. "That shade of green suits you," he said quietly. "It matches your eyes."

She didn't know how to handle a compliment like that from him. She laughed nervously. "Does it?"

He smiled slowly. It wasn't like any smile she'd ever had from him. It made his pale eyes glitter like sun-touched diamonds, made him look younger and less careworn. She smiled back.

Merrie joined them, an odd little smile touching her lips. "Having fun?" she asked Ivy.

"It's a very nice dance," Ivy replied, dragging her eyes away from Stuart.

"It is," Merrie agreed.

Hayes had been stopped on the way off the dance floor by a somber Harley Fowler, who motioned Cash Grier to join them. Hayes made a face before he rejoined them, disappointment in his whole look.

"We've had word of a drug shipment coming through," he said under his breath. "Harley was watching for it. He says they've got a semi full to the brim with cocaine. I have to go. We've been setting this sting up for months, and this is the first real break we've had." He stared at Ivy. "I can get one of my deputies to swing by and take you home," he began.

"She can ride with us," Stuart said easily. "No problem."

"Thanks," Hayes said. He grinned at Ivy. "Our first date and I blew it. I'll make it up to you. I promise."

"I'm not upset, Hayes," she replied. "You go do your job. There will be other dances."

82

"You're a good sport. Thanks. See you, Merrie," he added with a wink, nodding to Stuart as he headed for the front door.

Merrie was biting her lower lip, her eyes on Hayes's back as he left. Ivy noticed and didn't say a word.

"How about some of this punch?" Ivy asked her best friend. "It looks very good."

Merrie was diverted. "Yes. I'll bet it tastes good, too. But I want a word with Shelby Ballenger before I indulge. I'll be right back." She went toward Shelby. Ivy filled two glass cups with punch and handed one to Stuart.

He made a face. "It's tropical punch, isn't it? I hate tropical punch."

"They have coffee, too, if you'd rather," Ivy told him, putting the punch down on the table.

He met her searching eyes. "I would. Cream. No sugar."

She poured coffee into a cup, adding just a touch of cream. She handed it to him, but her hands shook. He had to put his around them, to steady them.

"It's all right," he said softly. "There's nothing to be afraid of."

She didn't understand what was happening to her. The feel of his big, warm hands around hers made her heart race. The look in his pale eyes delighted, thrilled, terrified. She'd never had such a headlong physical reaction to any other man, and especially not since that incredible night when he'd held her and kissed her as if he couldn't bear to let her go. It had haunted her dreams for more than two years, and ruined her for a relationship with any other man.

She let go of the cup with a nervous little laugh. "Is that enough cream?" she asked.

He nodded. He sipped it in silence while she sipped at her punch. The music was playing again, this time a slow, bluesy two-step.

Merrie came back to them, grinning. "I asked Shelby if she'd save me one of those border collies she and Justin are breeding. They're great cattle dogs."

Stuart scowled at her. "What the hell do you need with a cattle dog?"

"It's not for me," she replied. "There's a sweet little girl on my ward who has to have a tumor removed from her brain. She's scared to death. I asked her parents what might help her attitude, and they said she'd always wanted a border collie. It might be just what she needs to come through the surgery. You see," she added sadly, "they don't know if it's malignant yet."

"How old is she?" Ivy asked.

"Ten."

Ivy winced. "What a terrible age to have something so deadly."

"At least she'll have something to look forward to," Stuart added. "You really are a jewel, Merrie."

She made an affectionate face at him. "So are you. Now let's dance or eat or something so we don't burst into tears and embarrass Ivy."

He cocked an eyebrow and gave Ivy a mischievous look. "God forbid that we should embarrass her." He put down his coffee cup. "Dancing seems more sensible."

He took Ivy's glass of punch and put it down, only to draw her back onto the dance floor.

It was the sweetest evening of Ivy's life. She danced almost exclusively with Stuart, and he didn't seem to mind that people were watching them with fond amusement. It was well-known that Stuart played the field, and that Ivy didn't date anyone. The attention Stuart was showing her raised eyebrows.

Merrie didn't lack for partners, either, but she seemed subdued since Hayes had left. Ivy wondered if there wasn't something smoldering under Merrie's passive expression that led back to that old crush she'd had on Hayes.

When it came time to leave, Merrie informed Stuart that she was going to ride home with one of the Bates twins, who passed right by their house. She didn't give a reason, but Stuart didn't ask for one, either. He linked his fingers into Ivy's and drew her outside to his big, sleek Jaguar.

"I can't remember when I've enjoyed a party more," he remarked.

"It was fun," she agreed, smiling. "I don't get out much at night. Usually I'm trying to keep up with the accounts, including doing estimated taxes for all my clients four times a year. It keeps me close to home."

"You and Merrie have lost touch since she went to work in San Antonio."

"A little, maybe," she replied. "But Merrie is still the best friend I have. That doesn't go away, even when we don't see each other for months at a time."

He was quiet for a minute. "Have you heard from Rachel?" he asked.

She drew in a painful breath. "Yes. Last week."

"How was she?"

She wondered why he was asking her questions about her sister, whom he hated. "Pretty much the same, I guess." Except that she was steadily higher than a kite when she called Ivy, and she was running around with someone else's rich husband, she added silently.

He shot a glance at her. "That isn't what I hear."

Her heart welled up in her throat. She'd forgotten that he moved in the same circles as other rich, successful men. Rachel's garden slug of a boyfriend knew such people in New York. Stuart might even know Rachel's latest lover. "What do you hear?" she asked.

"That she's about to create a media sensation," he said flatly. "Which is why I brought Merrie to the dance. Hayes mentioned that he was bringing you, and I wanted to talk to you without the whole town knowing. Your boardinghouse isn't private enough, and my Mrs. Rhodes is a terrible gossip. That left me looking for a neutral spot. Here it is."

Her heart was hammering. Rachel again. It was always something, her whole life. Would she ever be free of her sister's messy problems?

"Don't look like that," he said curtly. "I know you

don't have any influence on her. I just don't want you to be surprised by some enthusiastic journalist out of the blue, asking you personal questions about your sister for print. Scandals pay well, especially if the victim's relatives can be shocked into a printable reaction."

She put her face in her hands. "How bad is it?" she asked.

"Bad enough." He pulled the car off the main road onto a dirt road and cut off the engine. When she looked around, disturbed, he added, "This is on my land. I don't want to sit in front of Mrs. Brown's boardinghouse and have curtains fluttering the whole time we're talking." He freed his seat belt and turned to her, one arm curved around the back of her bucket seat. "You need to know what you're up against before the story hits the tabloids."

She grimaced. Tippy Moore had gone through the tabloid mills before her marriage to Cash Grier. So had Leslie, Matt Caldwell's wife. She knew the devastating effect they could have on people's lives. But she never dreamed that she could become a victim of them. Surely Rachel's sister wouldn't be interesting news to anyone? On the other hand, Rachel had actually landed a few roles on Broadway, despite her drug habit, and one review had called her talent "promising." After years of auditions, it seemed that Rachel might actually make it as an actress. But Stuart looked uncomfortable.

"Tell me," she prodded gently.

"She's been supplying drugs to an elderly recluse who fancies himself in love with her," he replied curtly. "The problem is that he's recently married to a former beauty queen who doesn't want to share him and his fortune with anyone, least of all a minor actress with a drug dealer for a boyfriend. A mutual friend says she's about to go public with the story. If she does, it will ruin Rachel's chances of any more roles on Broadway, and it may put her drug-dealing boyfriend in prison. It might even put her there, if the wife decides to go public with what her very expensive private detective dug up on Rachel. She found a connection to some very big drug lords across the border; some of the same ones Hayes and Cash and Cobb of the DEA are trying to catch."

By now, Ivy was noticeably pale despite the semi-darkness of the front seats. That message Rachel had given her for the baker had been code, after all. Her sister was a drug dealer. Her heart ran away with fear. She pulled at a curl beside her ear. "I wonder if I could get lost in the Amazon jungle before Rachel gets it in the neck?"

"You'd have to come home one day. Running away never solved a problem."

She leaned back against the seat, sick to her soul. In a small town like Jacobsville, a tabloid story would be a gossip fest. There wouldn't be a place she could go where people wouldn't be talking about her.

She wrapped her arms around herself, feeling a sudden chill.

"Rachel told a lot of lies about you around town, when you were in high school," he said after a minute, his eyes narrow and thoughtful. "She fed me a dose of them, too. I actually believed her, until two years ago. But just the same, I made sure that she left town."

She felt her cheeks go hot, and she hoped he couldn't see. So that was why Rachel had gone away so suddenly, why her attitude toward Ivy had changed. She thought Stuart was protecting her little sister, and she was jealous!

"Copper Coltrain says that you were in his office frequently with injuries from 'falls' when you were in school," he persisted.

Her heart jumped. "I was clumsy," she said quickly.

"Bull! Your father drank to excess and Rachel fed him the same lies she fed other people about you," he countered. "She bragged about getting you in trouble with your father. It suited her to have you constantly out of favor, so that she'd inherit everything. Which she did."

The news that he knew all her problems, although she'd secretly suspected as much, made her sick. "Dad thought she was wonderful."

"Yes, and he was fairly certain that you weren't his child."

She gasped aloud, her eyes as wide as saucers. "What?!"

"I didn't think you knew that," he murmured, watching her. "Rachel said that your mother told her, before she died, that she'd had an affair and you were the result."

Of all the things Rachel had done to her, that was the absolute worst. She couldn't even find words to express how horrified she was. "Is it . . . is it true?" she asked unsteadily.

He was hesitant. "I don't know. There's an easy way to find out, if you want to know for sure. If you can get a hair from your father's brush, or if Coltrain has a blood sample from him on file, we can have a DNA profile done. If there isn't a sample, but if Coltrain has his blood type on file, we can have your blood typed. Paternity can be determined by blood groups. It won't prove anything for sure, unless we could get a DNA sample from your father, but it would at least show if you could have been your father's child."

"You'd do that, for me?" she asked, surprised at his indulgence.

"Of course," he said matter-of-factly.

It was a lot to swallow at once. No wonder her father had been so brutal to her! He thought she wasn't his child. And Rachel had used that knowledge—if it wasn't a lie—to cheat Ivy out of anything that belonged to her family. Rachel had inherited it all, and sold it all.

"She must hate me," Ivy said aloud.

"She was jealous of you," he corrected flatly.

"Oh, sure, I'm such a peach of a beauty, why wouldn't she be?" she asked sarcastically.

He reached out and tugged a lock of her hair. "Stop that. You're no ugly duckling, except in your own mind. But I wasn't talking about looks. Rachel was

90

jealous because of the way you are with people. You're always looking for the best in people, making them feel good about themselves, making them feel important. You never gossip or tell lies, and you're always around if anyone's in trouble or grieving. Rachel has never given a damn for anyone except herself. You made her feel inferior, and she hated you for it."

"She was beautiful," she said. "All the boys loved her."

"Even boys you tried to date," he added, as if he knew. He nodded. "Yes, I heard about that, too. Rachel delighted in stealing away any boy you brought home. She turned your girlfriends against you, everyone except Merrie. She told Merrie some whoppers about your social life." He looked away, his body stiffening. It didn't take a mind reader to know that Merrie had repeated the lies to him.

"I'm amazed you didn't forbid Merrie to have anything to do with me."

"I did," he said surprisingly, glancing at her. "She wouldn't listen, of course. And I stopped pressuring her about it when I realized how badly Rachel had lied about your character."

She knew what he was talking about, and it made her uneasy. He was remembering what a novice she was in a man's arms.

"Copper doesn't usually talk about patients," he continued. "But we're second cousins as well as good friends, and I've felt responsible for you since your father's death. He thought I should know about your home life. Just in case Rachel ever came down here and tried to start trouble. He didn't know I'd already gotten the news from a private detective I hired."

She couldn't look at him. It felt as if all the bruises and lacerations were plainly visible to anyone looking.

"You've never talked about it, have you?"

She shook her head. "Not even to Merrie."

"Merrie is more perceptive than you realize. She knew why you covered your legs when you went to school. You didn't want anyone to see the bruises he left on you with that doubled-up belt."

She bit her lower lip and looked up at him. She was remembering what Merrie had said about his own childhood, and how his father had punished him for refusing to give his life to football.

"You got your share, too, didn't you?" she asked quietly.

He hesitated for a moment. His dark brows drew together. "Yes," he replied finally. "I've never talked about it to anyone outside my family. The memories sting, even now."

"They would have locked my father up and thrown away the key if he'd done it today."

"Mine, too," he agreed. He smiled faintly. "Our fathers would probably be occupying adjoining jail cells." He sighed and traced a pattern at her throat, making her heartbeat throb. "Nobody's using a belt on my kids."

"Mine, either," she replied at once.

He smiled down at her. "We're all products of our upbringing. Pity we don't get to choose our relatives."

"You can say that again." She searched his eyes. "Rachel isn't afraid of anything except losing her chance to act in a starring role on Broadway. But if she gets caught up in a public scandal, it will kill her career stone dead. And she might go to prison for drug dealing. I don't know what she'd do if she had all that to contend with. She's not very strong emotionally."

"Only when she's on the receiving end," he agreed. "But she chose her own path, Ivy. We all do. Then we take the consequences of those choices."

She cocked her head. "What path did you choose that had consequences?"

"It was one I didn't choose," he said enigmatically. His hand slid under the silken fist of hair at her nape, warm and strong. "But we've done enough talking for one night."

As he spoke, he tugged her face gently under his. "Don't panic," he whispered against her mouth as his lips teased at it. "There are some things you just can't do in bucket seats . . ."

She went under in a daze of throbbing pleasure. It was like the first time he'd held her and kissed her, but much more explosive. The long years between kisses made her bold, made her hungry. She slid her arms around his neck and opened her mouth under his. He groaned. A shudder went through him. He hesitated, but only for a split second. Then he gathered her up whole and dragged her over the console and into his lap, and the kisses grew harder and more insistent.

She felt his big hand under the neckline of her gown,

gently tracing patterns down into the soft flesh under her bra. She gasped.

He lifted his head and looked into her wide, shocked eyes, with affectionate amusement. "Think of it as exploration into new territory," he teased gently. "You've got a lot of catching up to do."

"And you're offering to guide me through the under-growth?" she gasped.

"Frilly undergrowth," he murmured, looking down at the quick beat of her heart that was echoed in the trembling of her bodice as her pulse increased madly.

"I'm not sure," she began breathlessly.

"Neither am I," he agreed as he bent again to her mouth. "But it's been a long, dry spell and I've waited as long as I can and stay sane."

While she was trying to figure that out, his mouth opened on her parted lips and his hand trespassed right under her bra onto her soft flesh with a sureness and mastery that chased any thought of protest right out of her head. She clung to him and gave in to the sweetness of the moment.

CHAPTER SIX

JUST as Ivy was seeing stars, there was the purr of a big cat somewhere in the jungle of pleasure she was exploring.

Stuart must have heard it, too, because he raised his head and frowned as he looked into the rearview mirror. "I don't believe it!" he burst out.

She followed his gaze and saw flashing blue lights coming at breakneck speed right down the dirt road behind them.

"Hayes!" he muttered, and let out a word that made her blush. The all-white Jacobs County Sheriff's car pulled up past them, whipped around, and came back again, so that Hayes and Stuart were facing each other through open drivers' windows. In the time it had taken Hayes to turn around, Ivy had slid discreetly back into her own seat, straightened her clothing and smoothed her hair. She was grateful that it was dark, so that Hayes wouldn't be able to see the lingering traces of Stuart's demanding passion on her lips and hair.

"Aren't you a little far out of your territory?" Stuart drawled. "This is my land."

Hayes just stared at him. "We flushed a drug transport with three armed men inside," he said at once. "We got two of them, but one escaped not far from here. He's carrying an automatic weapon."

"Good God," Stuart exclaimed.

"I didn't think he'd be driving a Jag," he continued dryly, "but you can't rule out a carjacking. And this car was all alone in a field." He scowled. "What the hell are the two of you doing out here?"

"Talking about DNA profiles," Stuart shot back.

Hayes pursed his lips. "Oooookay," he said, but clearly not believing it. "Just the same, I'd take her home, if I were you. These guys don't play nice. One of my deputies is in the emergency room with a bullet in his hip."

"I hope you get them," Stuart said.

"Me, too. See you."

He roared away, sirens still going.

Stuart glanced wryly at Ivy. "I suppose we've talked enough for one night. I don't fancy fighting off drug dealers at this hour."

"Neither do I," she agreed, but there was disappointment about having to come down from the clouds. It had been a sweet few minutes.

"I'm not anxious to leave, either, Ivy," he said as he started the car. "But there's a time and place, and this isn't it."

With that enigmatic statement, he pulled the car back into the highway, and sped toward her boardinghouse. They arrived there too soon.

He got out of the car, opened her door and walked her to her front door. He noted the quick flutter of a curtain with an amused smile, and then positioned them where no windows intruded. He took her by the waist and looked down into her sad eyes in the porch light. "I shouldn't have told you about your father like that," he said apologetically. "I'm sorry."

"The tabloids wouldn't have been very kind about it, if I'd had to hear it from them," she said philosophically. "Thanks for the heads-up."

His big hands tightened on her small waist. "Go see Copper," he coaxed. "He'll do what he can to help you find out, one way or another. I'll take care of the bill. I'll tell him that, too," he added.

"All right."

"And don't worry yourself to death about your sister," he said firmly. "If the situation was reversed, I promise she wouldn't waste a night's sleep about you."

"I know that. But she's still the only family I have left in the world."

He drew in an audible breath. "That doesn't help, I'm sure." He bent and brushed his mouth gently over her soft, sensitized lips. She stood on her tiptoes to increase the pressure, shivering a little when he accepted the silent invitation and gathered her in close, so that they were riveted together, hip to hip.

She'd never known such pleasure. It felt as sweet as it had in his car, but much more intense. Her nails dug into the hard muscles of his shoulders as she gave in to the sheer delight of being close to him.

When she moaned, he drew back. His hands were briefly cruel as he fought the need to back her into the wall and devour her. He had to force himself to let her go.

She saw that, and was fascinated by the sudden change in him. It was so sweet to kiss him, beyond her wildest dreams of delight.

"We can't do much more of that," he whispered. "Not in public."

"Are we in public?" she whispered back, dazed.

He drew in a long breath. "If I don't stop kissing you, we're going to be. It's sweet, Ivy. Sweeter than my dreams."

"Sweeter than mine, too," she confessed, aching to have his mouth on hers again.

He knew that, but he had to be strong for both of them. It wasn't the place. He held her gently by the waist. "I have to fly to Denver for a conservation workshop. I'll call you when I get there."

She stared up at him with her heart flipping around. Her surprise was noticeable.

He searched her wide eyes. "Times change. So do people. You're twenty-one next month, aren't you?"

She nodded, spellbound.

He looked very somber for a minute. "Still years too young," he murmured as he bent his head. "But what the hell . . ."

He lifted her up against him and kissed her until her mouth felt bruised. She didn't complain. She held on for dear life, her arms tight around his neck, her feet just barely touching the floor at all. If this was a dream, she never wanted to wake up.

When she moaned softly, he put her back on her feet and let her go abruptly. His breathing was noticeably faster. "Stay out of trouble," he told her.

"I don't ever get into trouble," she replied dimly, her eyes on his hard mouth.

He smiled slowly. "Yes, but that was before."

"Before what?" she asked.

He bent and kissed her quickly. "Before me. Lock the door behind you."

He was walking away before she realized what he'd said. He was hinting at a new relationship between them. It made her breath catch in her throat. Her eyes followed him hungrily all the way to his car. He started it and turned on the lights, but he didn't budge. Finally she realized that he wasn't going until she was inside. She smiled at that protectiveness, which was so alien to their relationship. She waved, went inside and closed the door. Only when she turned off the porch light did she hear the car driving away.

Next morning at breakfast, Mrs. Brown and Lita were beaming at her, both affectionately amused.

"Have fun last night, dear?" Mrs. Brown asked. "I noticed that Sheriff Hayes didn't bring you home. Wasn't that Stuart York's car?"

"Yes, it was," Ivy confessed, and hated the warm color that blushed her cheeks. "Hayes had a call and had to leave."

"We heard on the radio that there was a shootout," Lita said. "Deputy Clark was admitted to the hospital with a gunshot wound."

"So was one of the suspects," Mrs. Brown said shortly. "They said Hayes got him."

"We saw him on the way home," Ivy confessed, but not how they'd seen him, or where. "He said the deputy was shot in the hip. He didn't mention the drug dealers getting shot, too."

"It was the one who went missing when they stopped the truck," Mrs. Brown said. "My daughter works as a dispatcher," she reminded the other women. "She said he was hiding in a chicken coop just off the highway. Hayes saw chickens flying out of the coop and went to investigate." She chuckled. "People shut their chickens up at sunset to keep them from getting eaten by foxes or raccoons. Nobody turns them out at night. Sure enough, there was this miserable little drug dealer, hiding there. He shot at Hayes and missed. Hayes didn't."

Ivy shook her head. "He takes so many chances," she said. "It will take a brave woman to marry him."

"Probably why no woman ever has," Lita remarked. "He was always a hothead, even when he was in high school. Always taking risks. He joined the police force when he was just seventeen. I guess his father influenced him."

"His father was a lovely man," Ivy remarked with a smile. "He loved flowers, did you know? He always had the most beautiful garden of them, and everybody thought it was his wife who did all the planting. But it wasn't."

"I'll bet Hayes doesn't raise flowers," Mrs. Brown remarked.

"He had a younger brother," Lita continued, frowning, "who died of a drug overdose. You know, they never found the person who bought him that bad batch of cocaine that did him in. They say that Hayes is out to get his brother's killer, that he'll never quit until the drug dealer goes to prison." She sighed. "He still thinks that Minette Raynor gave that drug to Bobby Carson, but I don't. Minette isn't the sort."

Ivy nodded. "I know, but he won't see it that way. He never stops once he's got a suspect in view. That's sort of scary, in a way."

"Makes me feel safe," Mrs. Brown chuckled. "I like knowing he doesn't let criminals get away."

"Me, too," Ivy had to admit. But she was thinking about Stuart and their changed relationship, going through the motions of eating and behaving normally. Inside, she was blazing with new hungers, new hope.

She went out to see her clients that day, but she was missing Stuart and waiting, hoping, for a phone call. She knew that he could have been joking. Maybe he'd just said it to tease. But the look in his eyes on the porch had been possessive, acquisitive. Her heart jumped every time she remembered how that last, desperate kiss had felt. Surely something so powerful had to be shared. After all, she hadn't been the only one breathing hard after the hungry kisses they'd shared. It was just that Stuart was older and more experienced. Maybe to him it was just a pleasant few minutes. To her, it was a taste of heaven.

Merrie called her at lunchtime, just to talk. Ivy was having a sandwich at Barbara's Café, but she didn't taste it. When the phone rang, she jumped to pull it out of her purse and answer it. It had to be Stuart. It had to be!

"Hi," Merrie said cheerfully.

"Oh. Hi," Ivy replied, trying to compose herself and not let her disappointment show. "How are you?"

"Lonely. You need to come spend a weekend with me," Merrie said. "I'm coming home next weekend. How about it?"

Once, Ivy would have jumped at the chance. Now, she was keeping secrets from her best friend. She didn't know whether she should agree. What she felt for Stuart might show, if she was under his roof. She didn't want Merrie to see it. Not yet. It was too new, too private, too precious to share. And what if he didn't want her around there at all? What if he'd just been playing some sophisticated game to which she didn't know the rules? Her insecurities floated to the top like cream in a churn.

"Ivy, you don't have to worry about me," Merrie said before Ivy could speak. Her tone was subdued, quiet. "I won't interfere."

"Excuse me?"

Merrie drew in a breath. "Hayes is a great catch."

Ivy was speechless. "Hayes?"

"He seems to like you a lot. He was really happy last night."

Now here was a problem she didn't know how to resolve. She couldn't admit that she was crazy about Merrie's brother, for fear that her friend might tease Stuart or do something to make him draw back from Ivy. On the other hand, she wasn't involved with Hayes and wasn't ever likely to be.

"Hayes is very nice," she compromised. "But he doesn't want to get serious about anyone, and neither do I. I don't want to get married for years yet. I want to enjoy being out on my own, and being single."

There was another sigh, but this one sounded strange. "Then, you're not involved with Hayes?"

"We're friends, Merrie. That's all."

"I'm glad," she said. "By the way, have you heard anything, about how he is?" Merrie added after a minute. "I heard that there was a shootout and someone got shot apprehending a drug dealer. Was it Hayes?"

"No!" Ivy said. "It was one of his deputies. One of the suspects got shot, too. Hayes is fine."

"Thank God."

"You've known Hayes a long time," Ivy recalled.

"Yes, since he used to stay with us when his father and mother had to go out of town to see about her parents in Georgia. Even though he was Stuart's friend, I always felt as if he were part of my family. He's a lot older than me, of course. Like someone I know in San Antonio," she added enigmatically.

The age difference between Merrie and Hayes was about the same as that between Stuart and Ivy. Stuart didn't seem to have a problem with it anymore, if his new attitude toward Ivy was any indication. So maybe there was hope for Merrie.

"He's not that much older, Merrie," Ivy said gently.

"Stuart thinks he is."

There was an edge in that usually calm tone. "He's your brother. He loves you. He just thinks . . ." She stopped at once.

"He thinks what?" Merrie prompted.

"He thinks that Hayes's profession puts him out of the running for you," she said reluctantly. "Hayes does take chances, Merrie. He can be a lot of fun, but under

103

it all is a man who takes risks, who walks right into gun battles. Stuart's just thinking about what's best for you."

"So that's what's been eating him lately," Merrie said dryly. "Old worrywart. But no relative, no matter how caring, can decide your life for you, you know."

"I know that. Merrie, Stuart loves you. He'd want you to marry someone you love."

There was a husky laugh. "Think so?"

"Yes."

"Well. That's something."

"You're very depressed. Why don't you come to the boardinghouse and have supper with us tonight? You know Mrs. Brown wouldn't mind. I could phone her."

"No. Thanks, anyway, but we've got a flu epidemic. I can't be spared, with so many health care workers out sick."

"Maybe when it's all over . . . ." She let her voice trail off.

"Yes. I'd love it."

"Take care of yourself," Ivy said. "And stop worrying about everything. Life evens out. Wishes come true."

"Sure they do," Merrie said cynically.

"I mean it. They do!"

Merrie sighed. "You always did believe in fairies."

"Angels, too, don't forget."

"If I have a guardian angel, he's asleep at the wheel."

"Stop that. Come and see me when you can."

"How about that invitation to spend the weekend?"

Merrie persisted. "You and Stuart weren't fighting, for a change, at the dance. You might enjoy it."

"I'll let you know," Ivy said, stalling. "I've got a new client."

"You and your blessed clients. Okay, then. Call me?"

"I'll call you. Take care, Merrie."

"You, too."

Ivy hung up. Poor Merrie.

She waited and waited, but there was no other phone call. She even checked to make sure the phone was working. By late evening, she was certain she'd misunderstood what Stuart had said. He was probably just joking. But he wasn't a man who usually cracked jokes.

She got ready for bed, climbed under the covers and was just about to turn out the light when the phone began to ring noisily.

Heart pounding, she leaped out of bed and upended her purse to find the small flip phone. She opened it with trembling hands and put it to her ear. "Hello?"

There was a deep, soft chuckle. "Dived for the phone, did you?"

She laughed breathlessly. "Yes," she confessed.

"I would have waited. I told you I'd call."

"Yes, but I thought maybe you got busy," she began.

"So you gave up on me."

She fidgeted on the bed. "Not really. Well, maybe. I wasn't sure that you weren't teasing."

There was a brief pause. "It's early days, isn't it,

Ivy?" he asked quietly. "We're only beginning to learn each other."

She wasn't sure what he meant. Her hand tightened on the phone. "Merrie invited me to spend the weekend."

"What did you tell her?"

"I said I'd let her know," she hesitated.

There was a short pause.

She felt insecure. "I didn't know if you'd approve."

The pause grew.

She felt her spirits hit the floor. She drew in a slow, shivery breath. "Stuart?"

There was a clink, like that of ice in a glass. "You don't know me at all."

"Of course I don't," she replied. "You've avoided me for two whole years."

"I had to," he said harshly.

She didn't understand what he meant. She was shy with him. It wasn't helping things.

He drew in another harsh breath. "Oh, hell." Ice sloshed in liquid again.

"I should go," she said sadly.

"Is it Hayes?" he asked harshly.

"What?"

"Are you in love with Hayes Carson?"

"I most certainly am not!" she exclaimed before she stopped to think.

There was a sigh. "Well, that's something, I guess." Another pause. "When I come back, we'll go for a drive and talk."

"That would be . . . nice."

"Nice."

She was lost for words. She loved the sound of his deep, slow voice. She didn't want him to hang up. But she didn't know what to say, to keep him talking.

"What are you doing?"

"Sitting on the bed in my nightgown, talking to a madman."

He burst out laughing. "Is that how I sound?"

"I feel like apologizing, but I don't know what for."

"I've had a long day," he told her. "We always get at least one tree hugger who comes to these conferences and demands that we set up special homes for our cattle where they can be properly housed and clothed and educated. This guy thinks we should learn to communicate with them."

She burst out laughing. "If you could, they'd say, 'don't eat me.'"

"You stop that," he muttered. "You know I don't raise beef cattle."

That was true. He had purebred Black Angus cattle. He knew the names and pedigrees of all his bulls, and they were as tame as dogs. The pedigree cows were treated almost as gently as the bulls. He was dangerous to cowboys who thought they could mistreat his livestock.

"I know that," she said gently. "What did you say to the tree hugger?"

"Oh, I didn't say anything to him."

There was an odd inflection in his voice. "But somebody else did?"

"One of the delegates from the national association invited him outside. The guy thought they were going to share a nice discussion. The delegate picked him up and put him down in the ornamental fountain."

She gasped. "But it's freezing in Colorado! There's snow!"

He chuckled. "I know."

"The poor man!"

"They gave him a blanket and a bus ticket," he said. "Last I saw of him, he was shivering his way back west into the sunset."

"That wasn't kind."

"Last year, it was a global warming advocate who said that we needed to find ways to stop cattle from belching and destroying the ozone layer. But I won't mention what happened to him."

"Why not?"

He only laughed. "You'll read all about it in the book he's writing. Last I heard, he was still looking for a publisher."

"Poor man."

"Poor man, hell. Humans belch as much as cattle do."

"I have never belched."

"Baloney," he shot back.

She sighed. "Well, I've burped quietly. But I never considered that it was doing damage to the planet."

He laughed. "I'm kidding. They actually let him present his program. One cattleman even bought him a drink."

"That was nice."

"It wasn't. The drink he bought him was a 'Wall-banger.'"

"What's that?"

"You wake up eventually with a hell of a hangover."

"You guys are terrible."

"I don't buy drinks for advocacy groups."

"You might influence them if you did."

"Not a chance." There was another pause. "I've got to go. There's someone at the door."

"An advocacy group?" she teased.

He laughed again. "No. A buddy of mine from Alaska."

"Does he raise cattle up there?"

"He's stationed at a military base there. Active military."

"Oh."

"I'll talk to you when I get back. Take care."

"You, too," she said, her voice softening.

"Good night, sugar."

He hung up before she was sure she'd really heard that. He'd never called her a pet name in all the time they'd known each other. It sounded as if they were actually going to be friends. Maybe even more. She slept finally in a welter of delightful, impossible dreams.

The next morning, her whole world fell apart. She answered her phone, thinking drowsily that it might be Stuart again, when a stranger addressed her.

"Miss Conley?" the voice inquired. And when she said yes, he continued, "I had this number from your police chief. I'm Sergeant Ed Ames, of the New York Police Department, Brooklyn Precinct. It's about your sister."

Her heart fell. "Is she all right?" she asked at once. "Has she been arrested?"

There was a loaded pause. "I'm sorry to tell you that she was found dead in her apartment this morning . . . Miss Conley? Miss Conley!"

She could barely breathe. She'd known this was coming, deep in her heart. But she wasn't ready to face it.

"Yes," she said heavily. "I'm still here. Sorry. It's . . . it's a shock . . ."

"I can imagine," he replied.

"You said she was found dead. Did she commit suicide?" she asked. "Or did someone else . . ."

"We don't know. There's going to have to be an autopsy, I'm afraid, to decide that. We'll need you to identify the body, to make sure it is your sister. Then someone has to arrange for disposition of her personal effects and her burial, or cremation."

"Yes. Of course. I'll have to come up there and deal with it." She hesitated, her mind spinning. "I'll come today. As soon as I can get a flight."

He gave her his telephone number and contact information. She wrote it all down and said goodbye.

She sat back down on her bed, rocking quietly with her arms wrapped around herself. Rachel was dead.

Rachel was dead. She hadn't even gotten to say goodbye. And now she had to go and deal with the funeral arrangements. Worse, she didn't even know if her sister had killed herself, or if someone had murdered her.

She thought of Jerry, her sister's drug-dealing boyfriend. Had he tired of her habit and killed her with an overdose? Had the millionaire's wife sent someone to kill her? Her head buzzed with all sorts of horrible images.

Then came the thought that she was all alone. Rachel had been the last living member of her family. The anguish of her sister's machinations and lies was over, but so was the last bond of kinship she had.

She thought of their father and wondered if he'd been there to meet Rachel when she crossed over. He'd loved the other sister so much. He hadn't loved Ivy. He didn't think Ivy was his. Was she? Had Rachel lied about that, too, as she'd lied about so many other things?

Maybe Rachel had left a note, a letter, something, to explain her hatred of Ivy. If she went to New York, maybe she could find it. Maybe she could understand the other woman, at long last.

She started packing.

CHAPTER SEVEN

LUCKILY, Ivy had enough in her savings account to cover a reduced fare round-trip airline ticket to New York. But once there, she would have expenses. She'd have to find somewhere to stay—she couldn't bear to stay at Rachel's apartment with the drug-dealing boyfriend lurking nearby—and there would be cab fare and then the cost of bringing Rachel home. It was a nightmare. If Stuart had been at home, she might have been bold enough to call him and ask for help. But it was too soon in their changing relationship for that.

On the other hand, she could call Merrie. But Ivy was too proud. It would sound as if she needed charity. No, she had to stand on her own two feet and do what was necessary. She was a grown woman, not a child. She could do this.

She'd never been on an airplane in her life. It was an adventure, from going through security to takeoff, which she compared in her mind to blasting off in a spaceship. She was sitting next to a nice elderly couple in tourist class. They were friendly, and seemed amused at her fascination with air travel.

Once at La Guardia, she took a cab to a modestly priced hotel that Lita had told her about, which was in Brooklyn, not too far from Rachel's apartment. She also had the number of the police sergeant who'd told her about her sister's death.

She checked in at the hotel and took time to go

upstairs with her single suitcase. The room was small, but neat and clean, and there was a lovely view of the city skyline. She wondered how she was going to bear the loneliness of it, though, after she went to the morgue to identify her sister's body. The ordeal was one she dreaded.

Sergeant Ames wasn't in his office when she got there, so she took a seat in the waiting room. The police precinct seemed in a constant case of chaos. People came and went. Lawyers came to see clients. Reporters came to talk to detectives. Uniformed officers came and went. It was a colorful mix of people, especially to Ivy, who was used to living in a town of only two thousand people. A few minutes later, a tall, dark-headed, good-looking man in a suit approached her.

"Miss Conley?" he asked, smiling.

She stood up. "Yes. Are you Sergeant Ames?"

"I am." They shook hands. "Sorry I was late," he added, leading her to his cubicle and offering her a seat. "I had to testify in a murder trial. Court just let out."

"Have you learned anything else about my sister's death?" she asked.

"Just that her boyfriend has a record as long as my desk," he replied curtly. "He has clients in high places around town. Apparently your sister was involved with one of them, a married man, and the client's wife was none too happy about the affair. She made threats against your sister's life. Then there's the boyfriend. A neighbor of theirs told one of our investigators that your sister and her boyfriend had frequent violent arguments. During their latest one, he told her to leave his client alone and she threatened to go to the police with information she said could convict him of drug smuggling." He folded his hands on the cluttered desk. "As you can tell, there's no shortage of suspects if it does turn out to be a case of murder." He frowned. "Is someone with you? Family? A boyfriend, perhaps?"

She shook her head. "I don't have any relatives, except Rachel," she replied. She thought about Stuart, but kisses didn't make relationships. "And no boyfriend," she added reluctantly. "There was no one I could ask to come with me."

He grimaced. "You're not going to try to stay in your sister's apartment?" he asked quickly.

"No," she told him. "I couldn't bear to stay there. I have a room in a small hotel for the night."

"Have you ever had to deal with a death in your family before?"

"My father died two years ago," she said. "But Rachel made all the arrangements. I just paid the bills. I don't know exactly what to do," she confessed.

"I'll walk you through the procedure," he said in a gentler tone. "What can you tell me about your sister's private life?"

"Probably no more than you know already," she said apologetically. "Rachel was older than me, and she didn't like me. She only got in touch with me when I could do something for her."

He studied her quietly. "You weren't close?"

She shook her head. "Rachel didn't want to live in a small town. She wanted to be an actress on Broadway." She felt a terrible emptiness in the pit of her stomach. "I knew that she used drugs. She's done that for a long time, ever since high school. But I never thought she'd die so young." Tears ran down her cheeks. "It's just been so sudden."

"May I make a suggestion?"

She wiped her eyes. "Of course."

"You said that you have a hotel room?"

"Yes," she replied.

"Go to it and rest for a couple of hours. Call me when you're ready and I'll take you to the morgue to identify her. How about that?"

She almost argued. But he was a kind man, she could see it in his dark eyes. She smiled. "I would like to do that. Thank you."

He stood up. "I'll have one of the guys drop you off at your hotel," he added, as if he knew how limited her funds were.

"Thank you," she said gently.

He smiled. "No problem. I'll see you later."

It wasn't even lunchtime yet. She wasn't hungry. The flight had taken away her appetite. She lay down on the bed covers and closed her eyes. The ordeal was still in front of her. But the sergeant had been right, a few minutes' rest might help her face the morgue.

She must have drifted off, because a persistent

knocking sound brought her back to the present. She climbed off the bed, wiping at her sleepy eyes, and went to the door. She looked through the peephole and couldn't believe her eyes.

She threw open the door and ran into Stuart's warm, strong arms. She held on for dear life, sobbing, so happy to see him that she couldn't even pretend.

"It's all right, honey," he said softly, drawing her into the room. He closed and locked the door and then lifted her, carrying her to the bed. He sat down on it and cradled her across his knees. "I know it's hard. Whatever else she was, she was still your sister."

"How did you know?" she sobbed into his shoulder.

"The cabdriver who took you to the airport is Mrs. Rhodes's second cousin. He phoned her and she phoned me." His arms tightened. "Why didn't you call me?" he asked. "I would have been there like a shot."

She didn't have that much self-confidence, especially where he was concerned. But miraculously, here he was. She'd never needed someone this much in her life. She wasn't alone anymore.

She cuddled up against him, shivering a little with relief. "I have to call Sergeant Ames and he'll take me to identify . . . identify the body."

"I'll do that for you," he said softly.

She looked up into his pale blue eyes. "I can do it," she said. "If you'll go with me."

He smiled. "Of course I will." The smile faded. "How did she die?"

"I don't know. The police aren't sure, either. He said

they'll have to do an autopsy to find the cause of death." She laid her cheek against his broad chest. "Her apartment will have to be gone through and her things removed. Then I have to decide whether to have her cremated or bring her home to Jacobsville and bury her there, near our parents."

"Rachel wouldn't have cared what you did with her," he said coldly.

"I'd really rather have her cremated," she told him sadly. She didn't want to mention that the expense of transporting a coffin to Jacobsville was too over-whelming for her. She was sure that Rachel had no health insurance, or life insurance. And even if she had, there was no doubt that Jerry would have had himself put on the policy as beneficiary. But that still left Ivy with the funeral expense.

"Then, we'll see about doing that," Stuart said after a minute. "But first things first. We'll go to the morgue, then we'll find a funeral home. After we've made the arrangements, we'll go back to her apartment and see what needs doing there."

"You make everything sound so simple," she remarked.

"Most things are. It's just a matter of organization."

She sat up on his lap, dabbing at her eyes. "Sorry. I just lost it when I saw you. I thought I'd have to do all this alone."

He pulled out a white handkerchief and put it in her hands. "Dry your eyes. Then we'll call your sergeant and get the process started. Okay?"

She smiled. "Okay."

Stuart tried to keep her from looking at Rachel, but she insisted. She wanted to see how her sister looked.

It was bad. Rachel was gray. There was no expression on her face, although it was pockmarked and very thin. She looked gruesome, but it was definitely Rachel.

Stuart and Sergeant Ames escorted her back to Ames's office, where they sat around his desk drinking cups of black coffee until Ivy was fortified enough to talk.

"We're going to have an autopsy done," Ames told them, "but the medical examiner says it's pretty conclusive that she died of a massive overdose of cocaine."

"Is that why she looks the way she does?" Ivy asked, dabbing at her eyes with Stuart's handkerchief. "I mean, her face looks pockmarked."

"That's the crystal meth she'd been using," he replied. "It's the most deadly drug we deal with these days. It ravages the user. A few months on it and they look like zombies."

"Why?" she asked suddenly. "Why would anyone use something like that in the first place?"

"People have been asking that question for years, and we still don't have an answer. It's one of the most addictive drugs," the detective told her gently. "Once it gets into their systems, people will literally kill to get it."

"How horrible," she said, and meant it.

"How long had she been using?" he asked Ivy.

"Since she was in high school," she told him dully. "I told my father, but he didn't believe me. He said Rachel would never do drugs." She laughed hollowly. "She'd come to see us when she was high as a kite, and my father never even noticed."

"Her father drank," Stuart interrupted solemnly. "I don't think he noticed much."

Ivy grimaced. "I never imagined she'd end up like this."

"What about her boyfriend?" Stuart wanted to know.

Ames shrugged. "We've managed to get a couple of convictions against him, but even so, he gets out of jail in no time, and goes right back to his old tricks. A couple of his clients are powerful figures in the city."

"On all the best television shows, the drug dealers go away for life," Ivy pointed out.

Ames chuckled. "I wish it was that way. It's not. For hundreds of reasons, drug dealers never get the sentences they deserve."

"When will they do the autopsy?" Ivy asked.

"Probably tonight," Ames said. "They don't have a backlog, for the first time in months. Once we have a cause of death, we can decide where to go from there."

"What about her apartment?" Ivy asked. "Is it all right for us to go there?"

"Yes," he replied and, reaching into his middle desk drawer, produced a key. "This is a copy of the key to her apartment, which we have in the property room. I thought you'd need access, so I had this one made. We've already processed her apartment."

"I'll need to clean it out and pack up whatever little family memorabilia she kept, so I can take it home with me," Ivy said dully.

"How well do you know Jerry Smith?" the detective asked her.

"I've seen him a few times," she replied. "I never liked him. I have migraine headaches," she added. "He came home with Rachel when our father died. I had the headache and he switched my medicine for some powerful narcotics. I realized he'd substituted something for my prescription pills, and I refused to take what he gave me. He thought it was funny."

Stuart looked murderous. "You never told me that," he accused.

"I knew what you'd do if you found out," she replied. "That man looks to me like he has some really dangerous connections."

"I have a few of my own," Stuart replied curtly. "Including two Texas Rangers, an FBI agent and our local sheriff. You should have told me."

She grimaced. "I was glad when Rachel and Jerry went back to New York."

"I'm not surprised," the sergeant said. "I have your sister's effects in the property room. If you'll come with me, I'll get them for you. You'll have to sign them out."

"All right." She stood up, feeling numb. "Thank you for being so kind."

"It goes with the job description," he assured her.

• • •

Stuart had hired a limousine. Ivy found it fascinating. She wished she wasn't so transparent to him. He seemed amused that she wanted to know everything about the expensive transportation.

He had the driver wait for them at Rachel's apartment building. He escorted Ivy up the stairs to the second floor apartment and opened the door. It was just the way Rachel had left it, except for the white outline that showed where her body had been.

Ivy was taken aback at the graphic evidence of her sister's death. She stood there for a moment until she could get her emotions under control. "I don't know where to begin," she said.

"Try the bedroom," Stuart suggested. "I'll go through the drawers in the living room."

"Okay."

She wandered into Rachel's bedroom, her eyes on the ratty pink coverlet, the scattered old shoes, the faded curtains. Rachel had always told everybody back home that she was getting good parts in Broadway plays and making gobs of money. Ivy had even believed it.

But she should have realized that Rachel wouldn't have been so persistent about their father's money unless she was hurting for it. A rich woman would have less need for a parent's savings.

Ivy opened the bedside table, feeling like a thief as she looked inside. There was a small book with an embroidered cover. A diary. Absently, Ivy stuck it in the pocket of her jacket and moved to the dresser.

There was hardly anything in the dresser except for some faded silk lingerie and underwear. The closet, however, was a surprise. Inside were ten exquisite and expensive evening gowns and two coats. Ivy touched them. Fur. Real fur. There were expensive high heeled shoes in every color of the rainbow on the floor of the closet.

She opened the jewelry box on the dresser and gasped. It could be costume jewelry, of course, but it didn't look cheap. There were emeralds and diamonds and rubies in rings and necklaces and earrings. It looked like a king's ransom of jewelry. What in the world had Rachel done to get all this, she wondered?

Stuart came in, his hands deep in his pockets, frowning. "She's got a big plasma television, a top-of-the-line DVD player and some furniture that came from exclusive antique shops. How did she manage all that without visible means of support?"

"That's a good question," Ivy replied. "Look at this."

Stuart looked over her shoulder at the jewels. He picked up a ring and looked at the inscription inside the band. "Eighteen karat gold," he murmured. "The stones are real, too."

"Do you think she stole them?" Ivy asked worriedly.

"I don't think it's likely that she owned them," he replied. "There's about a hundred thousand dollars worth, right here in this tray."

Her gasp was audible. "I thought it might be costume jewelry."

He tilted her chin up to his eyes. "You don't know a lot about luxury, do you, honey?" he asked softly. He bent and touched his mouth gently to hers. "I like you that way."

The touch of his mouth was almost her undoing, but she couldn't forget the task at hand. "Where do you think she got all this?" she persisted.

"If she was hanging out with a millionaire, I imagine he gave it to her."

"His wife will want it all back."

He nodded. "If she knows it's here." He frowned. "I'm surprised that Ames didn't take it and put it in the property room."

"Maybe he thought it was fake, too."

He chuckled. "No. That guy knows his business. He may have some sort of surveillance camera in here, waiting to see if anyone carries off the jewels."

"That's not a bad idea," she mused.

He closed the lid of the jewelry box. "No, it isn't." He checked his watch. "It's going on lunchtime. We can go back to my hotel and have room service send something up to us."

"I have my own room," she reminded him.

"We'll cancel it and pick up your suitcase," he replied. "I'm not letting you out of my sight," he added somberly. "Especially while we don't know exactly why your sister died."

She started to argue. He held up a hand. "I won't give up or give in. Just come along and don't fight it."

"You're very domineering," she accused.

"Years of working cattle has ruined me for polite society," he said with a twinkle in his pale eyes.

She laughed, as she was meant to. "All right," she said after a minute. She didn't mind being guided at the moment. She was worn. He picked up the jewelry box and put it in her hands.

"Her boyfriend will say these belong to him," he said. "But he's not getting them without a fight. We'll put them in a safe-deposit box for the time being."

"That's a good idea," she agreed. "He may not have killed her, but he helped her get where she is now. He shouldn't profit from her death."

"I agree."

On the way to the hotel, he stopped at a bank where he obviously had an account and asked for access to his own safe-deposit box. They deposited the jewelry box in it. He asked to speak to one of the vice presidents of the bank, who came out of his office, smiling, to motion Stuart and Ivy into it. Stuart asked him about funeral parlors in the city and was referred to a reputable one. The bank officer gave Stuart the number.

When they were back in the limousine, Stuart dialed the number and spoke to one of the funeral directors. He made an appointment for them later that afternoon to speak about the arrangements. The funeral home would arrange for transport of Rachel's body when the medical examiner released it. Then they went by Ivy's hotel and picked up her suitcase. Stuart, despite her protests, paid for the room.

"We can argue about it when we're back home," he told her.

His hotel room made hers look like a closet. It was a penthouse suite, one of those that figured in presidential visits, she guessed. Stuart took it for granted. He phoned room service and ordered food.

"You should have asked for more than that," he said when she was through a bowl of freshly made potato soup.

"It was all I thought I could eat," she said simply. "It hasn't been the best day of my life." She put down the spoon. "I don't think it's hit me yet," she added solemnly. "I feel numb."

"So did I, when my father died," he said, putting down his fork. He poured second cups of coffee for them both before he spoke again. "I was sure that I hated him. He'd spent his life trying to force me to become what he couldn't. But when it happened, I was devastated. You never realize how important a parent, any parent, is in your life until they're not there anymore."

"Yes," she agreed. "Nobody else shares your memories like a parent. My father was bad to me. He always preferred Rachel, and he never tried to hide it." She sighed. "Maybe it's a good thing that I know he didn't believe I was his child. It makes the past a little easier to bear. I wish I knew for sure, though."

"We'll find out. I promise you we will."

She stared at him across the table. "You must be letting deals get by while you're up here with me," she said.

He shrugged. "There's nothing any of my managers can't handle. That's why I hire qualified people, so that I can delegate authority when I need to."

She smiled. "I'm very glad. I could have done this by myself. But I'm glad that I didn't have to."

He finished his coffee and put his napkin on the table. His pale eyes caught hers from the other side of the table. "I'd never have let you go through this alone," he said quietly.

The words were mundane, but his eyes were saying things that made her heart jump up into her throat. A faint wave of color stained her cheeks.

He smiled slowly, wickedly. "Not now," he said in a deep, slow drawl. "We've got too much to do. Business now. Diversions later."

The blush went nuclear. She got up from the table, fumbling a little with her coffee cup in the process.

He laughed. She was as transparent as glass to a man with his experience. It made him feel taller to see that helpless delight in her face. He was glad he'd come to New York. And not just because Ivy needed help.

They sat in the funeral director's office, going over final arrangements for Rachel. Ivy decided on cremation. It was inexpensive, and Stuart had already mentioned that he was flying his own twin-engine plane home. There wouldn't be any problem with getting the urn containing Rachel's ashes through security.

She picked out an ornate black and gold brass urn. "I can have our local funeral director bury it in the space next to Daddy," she told Stuart.

"Some people keep the ashes at home," the director remarked.

"No, I don't think I could live in the house if Rachel was sitting on the mantel," Ivy said quietly. "My sister and I didn't get along, you see."

The director smiled. "I have a brother I couldn't get along with. I know how you feel."

They went back into his office and Ivy signed the necessary papers and wrote a check for the cost of the expenses, despite Stuart's protests.

Later, in the limousine, he voiced his disapproval. "You've got enough to do supporting yourself," he said curtly. "Rachel's funeral cost is pocket change to me."

"I know that," she replied. "But you have to understand how I feel, Stuart. It's my sister and my responsibility."

He caught her hand in his and held it tight. "You always were an independent little cuss," he mused, smiling at her.

She smiled back. "I like the feeling that I can stand on my own two feet and support myself," she replied. "I never had a life of my own as long as Rachel was alive. She was even worse than Dad about trying to manage me."

He pursed his lip. "Do I detect a double meaning?"

She laughed. "No. Well, yes. You do try to manage me." She stared at him curiously. "And I don't know why. You were just going around with some beautiful debutante. There was a photograph of you in a tabloid two weeks ago," she added and then flushed because that sounded like jealousy.

But he only smiled. "That photo was taken four years ago. God knows where they dug it up."

She blinked. "Excuse me?"

"The photograph was taken years ago. See this?" He indicated a tie tack that she'd given him for his birthday three years ago. "I always wear it with my suits. Look in the photo and see if you see it."

In fact, she hadn't seen it in that photo. It amazed her that he prized such an inexpensive present. And that he wore it constantly. "You like it that much?" she asked, diverted.

Instead of a direct answer, his hand slipped to her collar and dipped under it to produce a filigree gold cross that he'd given her for Christmas three years past. "You never take it off," he said, his voice deep and slow. "It's in every photo of you that my sister takes."

"I . . . it's very pretty," she stammered. The feel of his knuckles against her soft skin was delightful.

"Yes, it is. But that isn't why you wear it, any more than I wear the tie tack because it's trendy."

He was insinuating something very intimate. She stared into his pale eyes as they narrowed, and darkened, and her breath began to catch in her throat.

"We're both keeping secrets, Ivy," he said in a deep, soft tone. "But not for much longer."

She searched his pale eyes, looking for a depth of feeling that matched her own. He was familiar, dear. When she and Merrie were in high school, she'd felt breathless when he walked into a room. She hadn't realized, then, that the feelings she got when he was around were the beginnings of aching desire.

He traced the outline of her soft lips with his forefinger, making her tingle all over. He smiled, so tenderly that she felt she could fly. Any idea she'd had that he was playing a game with her was gone now. No man looked at a woman like this unless he cared, even if only a little.

CHAPTER EIGHT

IVY felt as if the ground had been pulled out from under her as she stared into Stuart's pale eyes. His gaze dropped to her soft, full mouth and lingered there until she thought her heart would burst out of her chest. She stared at his hard mouth and remembered, oh, so well, the feel of it against her own. The need was like a desperate thirst that nothing could quench. She started to lean toward him. His hand contracted. His face hardened. She could see the intent in his eyes even before he reached for her.

And just then, the car lurched forward as the traffic light changed, separating them before they'd managed to get close.

Ivy laughed breathlessly, nervous and shy and on fire with kindling desire.

He cocked an eyebrow. "You're safe," he murmured, although he still had her hand tight in his. "But don't get too comfortable."

She only smiled. His eyes were promising heaven. It seemed impossible that they'd been enemies for so long. This familiar, handsome, compelling, sexy man beside her had become someone she didn't know at all. The prospect of the future became exciting. But even as she felt the impact of her own feelings for him, she remembered why she was in New York City. Dreams would have to wait for a while.

They went back to Rachel's apartment to arrange things. Stuart went down to talk to the apartment manager. Ivy stayed in the apartment and began going through drawers again.

She found a photo album. She sat down with it on the couch and opened it. As she expected, the photos were all of Rachel. There was one of their father, sitting on the porch swing at his house. There were a few of their mother. There wasn't one single picture of Ivy anywhere in the album. It stung. But it wasn't unexpected.

She put the album aside and picked up a letter, addressed to Rachel and marked Private. It was trespassing. She felt guilty. But she had to know what was in the letter, especially when she read the return address. It was an expensive stationery, and the return address was that of a law firm in Texas.

Just as she started to open it, she heard footsteps. They weren't Stuart's. She stood up and slipped the letter into her slacks' pocket just as the door flew open.

Jerry Smith walked into the apartment as if he owned it. He was somber and angry. His narrow eyes focused on Ivy with something like hatred.

"What are you doing here?" Ivy asked coldly.

He shut the door behind him and smiled. The smile was sleazy, demeaning. He looked at Ivy as if she were a streetwalker awaiting his pleasure.

"So, it's the little sister, come looking for buried treasure, is it? Don't get too comfortable here, sweetheart. Everything in this apartment is mine. I paid for all this." He swept his arm around the room. "Mustn't steal things that don't belong to you," he added in a sarcastic undertone.

She would have backed down even a year ago. But she'd spent too much time around Stuart to cave in, especially when she knew he was nearby and likely to return any minute. This sleazy drug dealer didn't know that, and it was her ace in the hole.

"Any photographs and quilts and paintings in here are mine," she returned icily. "You don't get to keep my family heirlooms."

"Quilts." He made the word sound disgusting. "Rachel thought they were worth a fortune, because they were handmade. She took them to an antique dealer. He said they were junk. She tried to give them away, but nobody wanted them. She used them to pack her crystal in, for when she planned to move next month." He shrugged. "I guess she won't be moving anywhere."

Her relief at knowing the quilts weren't trashed disappeared when he made that odd statement. "Rachel never said anything about moving. Where was she moving to?"

"Back to your little hick town, apparently," he said. "She owned a house there."

"She didn't," Ivy returned, and felt guilty as relief flooded her. Rachel had planned to come home and let Ivy be her personal slave. "She sold the house two years ago."

"Whatever. She didn't remember much. I warned her about that damned meth. I don't even sell it, because it's so dangerous, but she got hooked on it and wouldn't quit."

"Did you kill her?" Ivy asked curtly.

"I didn't have to," he muttered. "She stayed comatose half the time, ever since she lost that big part she'd just landed in a play that's starting on Broadway in a couple of months. Her lover's wife knew the producer. She had him drop Rachel, then she called and told her all about it. She promised Rachel that she'd never get a starring role ever again. That was when she hit bottom."

"They're doing an autopsy."

He shrugged. "They usually do, when people die suddenly. I didn't kill her," he repeated. "She killed herself." He looked around, his eyes narrowing. "Don't take anything out of here until I have time to go through her things."

"I've already taken her jewelry to a bank for safe-keeping," Ivy returned.

"You've what?" He moved toward her, his hands clenched at his sides. "That jewelry is worth a king's ransom! She wheedled it out of that old man she was sucking up to!"

"Which means it belongs to him," Ivy replied.

"You'd really give it back to him, wouldn't you?" he taunted. "God, what an idiot you are! Tell you what, you give me half of it and I'll forget where it went."

"You can only bribe dishonest people," she said quietly. "I don't care that much about money. I only want to make a living."

"Rachel would have kept the lot!"

"Yes, she would have. She took and took and took, all her life. The only human being she ever cared about was herself."

"Well, you're not blind, are you?" He moved into the bedroom and opened drawers while Ivy hoped that Stuart would come back soon. Seconds later, Jerry barreled out of the bedroom. "Where is it?"

She blinked. "Where is what?"

"The account book!"

She frowned. "What account book? There wasn't any account book here!"

He went white in the face. "It's got to be here," he muttered to himself. He started going through drawers in the spacious living room, taking things out, scattering them. "It's got to be here!"

She couldn't understand what he was so upset about. Obviously there would be some sort of record of rent and other expenditures, but who kept a journal in this day and time?

"Wouldn't it be on the computer?" she asked, indicating the laptop on the dining room table.

"What? The computer?" He turned on the computer

and pulled up the files, one by one, cursing harshly as he went along. "No, it's not here!" He stared at her over the computer. "You took it, when you took the jewelry, didn't you?" he demanded. "Did you get my stash, too?"

He strode into the bathroom. Loud noises came from the room. He appeared again with some small bags of white powder. "At least only one is missing," he said, almost to himself. He stuffed the bags into his pants pockets. He glared at Ivy. "I don't know what your game is, but you'd better find that journal, and quick, if you know what's good for you."

"What journal?" she demanded. "For heaven's sake, my sister just died! I'm not interested in your house-hold accounts!"

He glared back.

"Did she have any life insurance?" she asked, forcing herself to calm down. "A burial policy?"

"She didn't expect to die this young," he returned. "No, there's no life insurance." He smiled coolly. "You can leave the apartment and its contents to me. Now take whatever you want of her 'heirlooms,' and then get the hell out of this apartment."

She wanted to argue, but Stuart would be here soon, and after Jerry got his comeuppance, he wasn't likely to let her back in again. She retrieved the quilts out of the closet, leaving the crystal stacked neatly on the floor. She took the photo album, although the photos were mostly of Rachel. She took none of the dresses or gowns or shoes or furs. Rachel's whole life boiled down to frivolous things. There wasn't a single book in the entire apartment.

Clutching the quilts and the photo albums, she moved back into the living room, where Jerry was still pulling open drawers, looking for the mysterious journal.

He seemed surprised when he saw what she had. "There were evening gowns in the closet. Weren't you interested in them? You and Rachel were almost the same size."

"I can buy my own clothes," she replied. It was a sore spot. Just once, when she was sixteen, she'd asked to borrow one of Rachel's gowns to wear to the prom. Rachel had asked why, and Ivy had confessed that a nice boy from the grocery store had invited her to the prom. So when he came to the house, Rachel had flirted with him and before he left, Rachel had teased him into driving her to Houston to see some friends on the same night as the prom. Then Rachel had mocked Ivy about borrowing the gown, adding that she hardly needed one since she no longer had a date.

"Did Rachel send you anything to keep for her?" Jerry persisted.

"Rachel only phoned me when she wanted me to send her something," she replied. "She wouldn't have trusted me with anything. She never did."

"Yeah, she said you stole her stuff when she was living at home."

Ivy's face went red with bad temper. "I never took anything of hers. It was the other way around. She could tell a lie to anyone and be believed. It was her greatest talent."

"I guess you were jealous of her, because she was so beautiful," he replied.

"I'm not jealous of people who don't have hearts."

He laughed coldly. "Beauty makes up for character."

"Not in my book."

He moved toward her, noting her quick backward movement. He smiled tauntingly. "Maybe you and me could get together some time. You're not pretty, but you've got spirit."

"I'd rather get together with a snake."

He lifted an eyebrow. "Suit yourself. I guess you'll grow old and die all alone in that hick town you come from." He touched her long, blond hair. "You could have some sweet times if you stayed here with me."

The door flew open and Jerry's face went rigid as the tall, dangerous man saw what Jerry was doing, stalked right up to him, took his hand from Ivy's hair and literally pushed him away.

"Touch her again and I'll break your neck," Stuart said, his whole demeanor threatening.

"Hey, man, I'm cool!" he said, backing even further away with both hands raised, palms out.

The flippant, cocksure young man of seconds before was flushed with nerves. Ivy didn't blame him. Stuart in a temper was formidable. He never lost control of himself, but he never flinched when confronted. The meanest of his cowboys walked wide around him on the ranch.

Ivy felt relief surge up inside her. Instinctively she moved closer to Stuart—so close that she could feel his strength and the warmth of his body. His arm slid around her shoulders, holding her near. She felt safe.

"I was just telling Ivy that this stuff is mine," Jerry said, but not in a forceful tone. "My money paid for it."

"And I told him," Ivy replied, "that all I wanted was whatever heirlooms from my family that Rachel kept here. I've got them . . . three quilts and a photo album." She was holding them.

"Ready to go?" Stuart asked her calmly, but his cold eyes were pinning Jerry to the wall.

"Yes," she said.

"All right, then."

She grabbed her purse from the table and went through the doorway. Stuart gave Jerry one last, contemptuous look before he closed the door behind them.

"The drug dealer, I take it?" he asked, relieving Ivy of the quilts.

"Yes. He was being very nasty until you showed up. Thanks for saving me."

He chuckled. "You were doing pretty well on your own, from what I saw." He led the way into the elevator and pressed the button for the lobby. "At least you won't have to dispose of the apartment and its contents."

"Yes, that's one worry gone." She looked up at him. "He was desperate to find some sort of account book he said Rachel had. He was frantic when he couldn't locate it."

"Did you find it?" he asked.

She shook her head. "There weren't any account books that I could see. He was furious about the jewelry, too," she added.

"He can try to get them back, if he likes. I have some great attorneys."

"I told him they were going back to the millionaire who gave them to her," she replied.

He laughed. "That must have given him hives."

"He was upset. I meant it, though." She grimaced. "But how am I going to find out who he is?"

"I'll take care of that," he said, so easily that Ivy relaxed. "All you have to worry about is the funeral. And I'll help with that."

"You've been so kind," she began.

He held up a hand. "Don't start."

She smiled. "Okay. But thanks, anyway."

"I couldn't leave you to do it alone." He led her out of the elevator when it stopped and out to the limousine, which was waiting for them just beyond the entrance. Stuart motioned to the driver and he pulled out of his parking space and around to the front of the apartment building.

The quilts were placed in the trunk and Stuart helped Ivy into the limousine.

They went back to the hotel. Ivy felt drained. She hadn't done much at all, but the stress of the situation was wearing on her nerves.

"You can have the master bedroom," he offered. "I'll have the one across the living room . . ."

"But I don't need all that room," she protested. "Please. I'd really rather have the smaller of the two."

He shrugged. "Suit yourself." He put her suitcase onto the bed in the smaller room and left her to unpack. "Why don't you lie down and rest for a while? I've got some phone calls to make. Then we'll see about supper."

"I haven't got anything fancy with me," she said as she opened the suitcase. "Oh, no," she muttered, grimacing as she realized that she'd only packed another pair of slacks and two blouses and an extra pair of shoes. She'd forgotten that she was going to spend the night.

"What's wrong?" he asked.

"I didn't pack a nightgown . . ."

"Is that all?" He pursed his lips, letting his eyes slide down her body. "I can take care of that. You get some rest. I'll be back in a little while. Don't answer the door," he added firmly. He didn't add why. He was sure the tabloids would pick up the story, and some enterprising reporter could easily find out that Ivy was in town to see to her sister's burial arrangements. He didn't want Ivy bothered.

"I won't answer the door." She wanted to offer to give him some money to get her a nightgown, but she didn't have it. The airfare and taxis had almost bankrupted her.

He was gone before she could even make the offer. She kicked off her shoes and put the open suitcase on the folding rack. Then she sank down onto the comfortable bed, in her clothes. She didn't mean to doze off, but she did. The long day had finally caught up with her.

She woke to the smell of freshly brewed coffee. She started sitting up even before she opened her eyes, and a deep, masculine chuckle broke the silence.

"That's exactly how I react to fresh coffee when I've been asleep," he murmured, standing over her with a cup and saucer. The cup was steaming. He handed it to her. "Careful, it's hot."

She smiled drowsily as she took it. The color told her that he'd poured cream in it. He'd remembered that she only liked cream in her coffee. It was flattering. It was exciting. So was the way he was looking at her.

"Hungry?"

"I could eat," she replied.

"I had room service send up a platter of cold cuts," he told her. "Come on in when you're ready."

She took a minute to bathe her face and put her hair back up neatly before she joined him in the suite's living room. The tablc held a platter of raw vegetables with several dips, as well as cold meats, breads and condiments.

"Have a plate." He offered her one. "I like a steak and salad, but it's too late in the day for a heavy meal. Especially for you," he added, studying her. "You need sleep."

She grimaced. "I haven't really slept since this happened," she confessed. "I always knew Rachel could overdose. But she'd been using drugs for years without any drastic consequences."

"Anyone can take too many pills," he said, "and die without meaning to."

"Yes, like Hayes Carson's brother did," she remarked. "Hayes still isn't over that, and it's been years since his brother died."

He didn't like the reference to Hayes, and it showed. He didn't answer her. He loaded a plate and sat down with his own cup of coffee.

She sat at the table alone, nibbling on food she didn't taste. He was more taciturn than usual. She wondered why the mention of Hayes set him off like that. Perhaps they'd been rivals for a woman's affection. Or maybe it was just because he didn't want to see his sister get serious about Hayes.

"He's not a bad person," she ventured.

He glowered at her. "Did I say that he was?"

"You can't tell Merrie who to date," she pointed out.

He looked totally surprised. "Merrie?"

"She and Carson are friends," she persisted. "That doesn't mean that she wants to marry him."

He didn't answer. He frowned thoughtfully and sipped coffee.

She didn't understand his odd behavior. She finished her food and her coffee. She was worn-out, and the ordeal wasn't over. She still had the cremation ahead of her. There was something else, too. She would be truly alone in the world now. The thought depressed her.

"Are you going to call that man about the jewelry Rachel had?" she asked.

He nodded. "Tomorrow. We'll get everything else arranged then as well." His eyes narrowed. "I'm curious about that ledger Rachel's boyfriend mentioned."

"Me, too," she said wearily. "If he wants it that bad, it must have something to do with his clients."

He didn't say anything immediately. He looked thoughtful, and concerned. "I've heard it mentioned that Rachel knew where to buy drugs in Jacobsville. We both know that it's been a hub for illicit drug trafficking in the past. It still is." He frowned. "That ledger might have some incriminating evidence in it, and not just about Rachel's boyfriend." He stared at her. "You don't have any idea what it looks like?"

She shook her head. "I didn't ask. He was being obnoxious." She smoothed back her hair. "I wish I could feel something," she said dully. "I'm sorry she died that way, but we were never close. She did everything she could to ruin my reputation. I used to think we might grow closer as we aged, but she only got more insulting."

"Rachel liked living high," he said. "She didn't care how she achieved status."

There was something in his tone that made her curious. "She was in your class in high school, wasn't she?"

"Yes." His dark eyes narrowed. "She made a play for me. I put her down. She was vengeful, and you and Merrie were best friends."

That explained why Rachel had suddenly turned

against Ivy; she thought Ivy's friendship with Merrie gave her access to Stuart. If Rachel had wanted Stuart, it must have galled her that Ivy was welcome in his house. Rachel might even have guessed how Ivy felt about him, which would have given her a motive to try to convince Stuart that Ivy was promiscuous.

"So she set out to make you think I was running wild," she guessed.

He grimaced. "Yes, she did. I'm sorry to say she might have succeeded, except that Merrie knew you and defended you."

She smiled. "Merrie was always more like a sister to me than Rachel ever was."

"She likes you, too." He got up. "Bed. You need rest."

She hesitated.

He guessed why and chuckled. "I didn't forget." He produced a bag from Macy's and handed it to her. "Sleep well."

"I'll pay you back," she said with determination.

He shrugged. "Suit yourself. Good night."

"Good night." She hesitated at the door to her room. "Stuart . . . thanks. For everything."

"You'd do the same for anyone who needed help," he replied easily.

She smiled. "I guess so."

She went into her room and closed the door. When she opened the bag, she caught her breath. He'd purchased a gown and peignoir set for her. The gown was pale lemon silk with white lace trim, ankle-length, with a dipping bodice and spaghetti straps. The peignoir had long sleeves and repeated the pattern of the gown. She'd sighed over similar styles in Macy's herself and dreamed of owning something so beautiful. It was even prettier than the set Merrie had loaned her that long-ago night. She'd never have been able to afford something like this on her budget. She didn't know how she was going to repay Stuart for it, but she had to. She couldn't let him buy something so intimate for her.

She put on the ensemble and brushed out her blond hair so that it haloed around her shoulders and down her back. When she looked in the mirror, she was surprised at how sensual she looked. That was a laugh. What she knew about men would fit on the back of an envelope.

She climbed into bed and turned out the light. She wished she had something to read. She wasn't even sleepy. Her mind went back to the sight of Rachel in the morgue. She forced the memory out and replaced it with lines from a book she'd read about meteorites. That amused her and she laughed to herself. Stuart probably didn't know how fascinated she was about the space rocks, or that she was constantly borrowing books from the library about their structure. She loved rocks. She had boxes of them at her apartment. Everyone teased her about their number and variety. She was forever looking for anything unusual. Once she walked right out into a plowed field to search for meteorites and came away with projectile points instead.

Merrie said she should be studying archaeology, and Ivy had replied that chance would be a fine thing.

Even if she didn't study it formally, she knew quite a lot about the subject. Everyone should have a hobby, after all.

She closed her eyes and thought about the projectile points. She'd taken them to a professor of anthropology at the community college, who'd surprised her by dating them at somewhere around six thousand years old. It had never occurred to her that they were more than a hundred years old. That prompted her to get more books from the library about projectile points. She was surprised to learn that you could date them by their shape and the material from which they were made.

She thought back to the summer she was eighteen. Stuart had been out on the ranch with his cowboys rounding up the bulls, to move them to greener pastures. She'd watched him stand up in the saddle and ride like the wind. The picture had stayed with her when he'd come in for lunch. He had seen her rapt attention as he'd swung down out of the saddle with lazy grace.

He'd looked at her in a curious way, his pale eyes glittering. "Staring at me like that will get you in trouble," he'd said in a deep, slow tone.

She'd laughed nervously. "Sorry. I love to watch you ride," she'd added. "I've never seen anybody look so much at home in the saddle."

He'd given her a strange look. "I did rodeo for several years when I was in my teens," he'd said.

"No wonder you make it look so easy."

He'd reached out and touched her soft hair. His eyes had been intent on her face, and he hadn't smiled. Some odd magnetism had linked them at that moment, so that she could hardly breathe. Even now, almost three years later, she could still feel the pure intensity of that look he gave her. It was when she'd realized how she was starting to feel about him.

For just a few seconds, his pale eyes had dropped to her soft mouth and lingered until she flushed. She waited, breathless, for his head to bend. And it had started to. Then one of the cowboys had called to him. He'd walked away as if nothing at all had happened. After that, he'd avoided Ivy. Right up until that fateful night she'd spent with Merrie in a borrowed lemon-colored gown . . .

Somewhere music was playing softly. Perhaps Stuart had the radio on in the adjoining part of the suite. It was sweet music, sultry and slow. As she listened to it, she began to drift away.

She was a little girl again, running out through the fields around the house where she'd grown up. She was wearing jeans and an old white shirt and, as usual, she searched for unusual rocks.

Behind her, Rachel was dancing around in a full white gown and high heeled shoes, singing off-key and stumbling around.

Ivy turned and called to her, cautioning her about the sudden deep crevasses in the field. Rachel made a face and replied that she knew what she was doing. Just then, she tripped and fell into one of the deep trenches.

Ivy ran toward her. Rachel was hanging on to a small bush at the edge of the crevasse, screaming at the top of her lungs.

"If I fall, I'll tell everyone that you pushed me!" she threatened.

"I'll save you, Rachel!" Ivy shouted. "Here. Grab my hand!"

"Your hands are dirty," Rachel shouted back. "Dirty, dirty, dirty! You're dirty. You aren't my sister! I hate you! Go away! Go away!"

"Rachel, please . . ." she pleaded.

But Rachel jerked her hand back. She made a rude gesture with her hand and leaned back, falling deliberately into the darkness below.

"You killed me, Ivy. You killed me!" she yelled as she fell faster. Then there was a scream, piercing and terrifying. It went on and on and on . . .

CHAPTER NINE

"Ivy. Ivy! Wake up!"

Strong hands held her by the wrists. She was being lifted, higher and higher. Rachel had fallen to her death, but this determined voice wouldn't let Ivy follow her. She took a deep breath and slowly opened her eyes.

Stuart's eyes were there, filling the world. She blinked sleepily.

"Wake up, sweetheart," he said gently. "You were having a nightmare."

She searched his face. "Rachel wouldn't let me help her. She fell into a crevasse. I couldn't save her."

His hands became caressing on her wrists. "It was only a dream. You're safe."

"Safe."

His gaze dropped to her bodice and his face seemed to clench. "You're sort of safe," he amended.

She was awake now, and she realized suddenly why Stuart was staring at her like that. Her bodice had dropped so that one of her pretty, firm breasts was on open display. Stuart had a ruddy color across his high cheekbones and his teeth were clenched, as if he were exerting maximum self-control.

"You . . . you shouldn't look at me, like that," she stammered as color shot into her own cheeks.

"I can't help it," he said huskily. "You have the most beautiful breasts I've ever seen, Ivy."

She couldn't have uttered a word to save her life. He knew it, too. His big hands let go of her wrists and took her by the shoulders instead. His thumbs eased the tiny straps over her shoulders and down her arms. The bodice fell to her waist.

He was only wearing silk pajama bottoms. His broad, hair-covered chest was almost touching her bare breasts.

"As I recall," he whispered, "this is about where we left off, two years ago. I even got the color of the gown right."

He had, but she couldn't answer him. She couldn't breathe. The clean, sexy scent of his body wafted up into her nostrils. She felt his breath against her lips as his hands became lightly caressing on her upper arms. The tension between them twisted like cord. Ivy trembled all over as the slow, exquisite pleasure began to grow.

"What the hell," he whispered at her mouth. "It's this or go crazy . . ."

His mouth opened on her soft lips in a hard, insistent pressure that held traces of desperation. His arms swallowed her, grinding her bare breasts against the warm muscles of his chest.

She moaned jerkily at the rush of sensation.

He hesitated. "Did I hurt you?" he whispered.

"Oh, no," she whispered back, shyly lifting her arms around his neck. "I didn't know . . . it would feel like this."

He smiled slowly. "Didn't you?" He bent again, but this time his mouth was less desperate. It was tender, teasing. He nibbled her lower lip and smiled again as she parted her lips to lure him closer. His thumb probed gently, coaxing her mouth to open. When it did, his tongue slowly trespassed inside. "No, don't fight it," he whispered against her lips. "It's as natural as breathing . . ."

She felt him lift and turn her, so that she was lying on her back. His powerful body eased down over hers, one long leg insinuating itself between both of hers over the gown.

She stiffened, wanting more and afraid of it, all at once.

He lifted his head and searched her wide, apprehensive eyes. He brushed the hair back from her temples. His body was half over her and half beside her on the wide bed. But he didn't seem to be in a hurry. He bent and brushed his mouth over her eyelids, closing them. She felt her breasts go tight, pressed so hard up against him. She was aching for something she didn't understand.

He seemed to know it. "Ivy?"

"What?" she managed shakily.

"Lie back and think of England," he murmured wickedly.

A laugh jerked out of her tight throat.

He lifted his head, grinning down at her. He propped on an elbow while his other hand began to trace lightly, boldly, around a distended nipple. "Or, in our case, lie back and think of Texas." He bent again, brushing his open mouth along her collarbone. He felt her body shudder. He smiled against her soft skin as his mouth slowly trespassed down, close to but never touching the nipple. She began to twist helplessly as the sensations overwhelmed her. She was new to this kind of physical pleasure. Her reactions were unexpected, even to herself.

Her short nails bit into his shoulders as his mouth teased at her breast.

"You haven't done this before," he murmured, savoring her response.

"No," she agreed. She shivered as his mouth grew slowly insistent. "Stuart . . . !" she ground out as his lips traced very lightly closer and closer to the nipple.

"What do you want?" he whispered against her breast. "Tell me."

"I . . . can't," she moaned.

His hand slid under her, lifting her hips up against the slowly changing contour of his powerful body. "Tell me," he coaxed. "You can have anything you want."

She moaned aloud. "You . . . know!"

"Stubborn," he pronounced. He lifted his head to look down into her misty, fascinated eyes staring blindly up at him. Her whole body was trembling with passion. "You can't imagine how badly I've wanted your breasts under my mouth, Ivy," he told her as his gaze fell to her bodice. "But even in dreams, it was never this good." He moved closer. "I like feeling you tremble when I do this," he whispered as his mouth began to open on the soft flesh. "But it's going to be like a jolt of lightning when I do what you really want me to do . . ."

As he spoke, his warm mouth moved right onto the nipple and pressed down, hard.

She arched off the bed, crying out. Her whole body shuddered as the pleasure bit into her. She clutched him helplessly, whimpering as his mouth became demanding.

He rolled onto her, nudging her long legs out of the way so that she could feel him from hip to breast in an intimacy that burst like sensual fireworks in her body.

"Yes," she groaned. "Please, Stuart, please . . . !" Her voice rose as he pressed her down into the mattress. "Oh, please, don't stop!"

His mouth slid up to cover hers, devouring it, possessing it, as his body moved sensuously over hers. She hung on for dear life. She was losing it. She wanted him. She wanted him so badly that it was almost painful when he suddenly rolled away from her and got to his feet.

She lay there, bare to the waist, shivering in the aftermath, too weakened by her own surrender to even manage to cover herself. She stared at his long back, watching him fight to regain control.

After a minute, he took a long, shuddering breath, and then another, before he turned. He stared at her hungrily, his eyes making a meal of her as she lay there, bare-breasted, her hands by her head on the pillow. He stood over her with eyes that burned like dark fires.

She moved helplessly on the bed.

"No," he said quietly. "There's a time and place. This isn't it."

"You want to," she said with new knowledge of him.

"Good God, of course I do!" he ground out. "I hurt like a teenager after his first petting session. Just for the record, I don't seduce virgins. Ever."

She drew in a short, jerky breath. "How do you know . . . ?"

"Don't be absurd," he interrupted.

Which meant that she was as transparent as glass to

him, with his greater experience. Oddly she didn't feel embarrassed or self-conscious. He was looking at her boldly, and she loved his eyes on her body.

"I ache all over," she whispered.

"So do I." He sat down beside her and blatantly traced her breasts with the tips of his fingers. "I could do anything I wanted to you. But in the morning, you'd hate both of us."

It was the truth. She wished it wasn't. "Everybody else does it. They had a poll . . ."

"Polls can be manipulated." He bent and put his mouth tenderly against her breasts. "Virginity is sexy," he whispered. "I lie awake nights thinking about how I'd take yours."

She flushed.

He laughed. "Tell me you've never thought about doing it with me," he dared.

The flush got worse.

He drew in a long breath. "One of us has to be sensible, and I'm giving up on you," he mused, watching her body move on the sheets. "Come here."

He slid under the covers and tucked her close against his side. He turned out the light and cuddled her closer. "You can take my word for the fact that I'm violently aroused and desperate for relief. So just lie still, recite multiplication tables and try to sleep."

"You're staying?" she whispered, fascinated.

"Yes. And you won't have any more nightmares. Now go to sleep."

She closed her eyes. She was sure that she couldn't

sleep with his warm, powerful body so close to her. But she drifted off almost at once and slept until morning.

When she woke, it was to a throbbing pain in her right eye and nausea that made her lie very still. The headache wasn't unexpected. Stress often combined with other factors to cause them.

Stuart came in with a cup of coffee, but he stopped smiling when he saw Ivy holding her head and pushing against her right eye. "Migraine," he murmured.

She nodded, swallowing hard to keep the nausea down. "I'm so sorry."

"Don't be ridiculous, you don't plan to have headaches. Lie back down."

When he came back, scant minutes later, he had a doctor with him. The doctor smiled pleasantly, asked her a few questions, listened to her heart and lungs and popped a shot into her arm. She closed her eyes, unable even to thank him, the pain was so severe. She eventually dozed off.

The second time she awoke, the pain had reduced itself to a dull echo of its former self. She sat up, drowsy, and smiled at Stuart.

"Thanks," she said huskily.

"I know how those headaches feel," he reminded her. "Can you eat some scrambled eggs and drink some coffee?"

"I think so." She got out of bed and staggered a little from the drugs. "It was just all the pressure," she added. "I always get headaches when I'm under stress."

"I know. Come on." Instead of letting her walk to the table, he swung her up in his arms, in the pale gown, and carried her there. He sat down with Ivy in his lap, within reach of the late breakfast he'd ordered, and began to spoon-feed her eggs and bacon.

She was amazed at the transformation of their relationship, as well as his sudden tenderness. She reacted to it hungrily, never having had anyone treat her so gently in all her life.

He smiled down at her, his dark eyes soft and full of strange lights. When he finished, he cuddled her close and shared a cup of coffee with her. Neither of them spoke. Words weren't even necessary. She felt safe. She felt . . . loved.

Later, the limousine took them to the funeral home where Rachel's cremated remains were already interred in an ornate bronze urn. The limousine took them from there to the airport, where Stuart's pilot was waiting to fly them home in the Learjet.

It was like a beginning. He held hands with her on the jet. When they loaded her few possessions into his car, which had been left parked at the airport, he held her hand as he drove toward her boardinghouse.

She didn't question it. The feeling was too new, too precious. She was afraid that words might shatter it.

He pulled up in front of Mrs. Brown's house and cut the engine. He helped her out first, then he carried her suitcase and her bags of quilts and photo albums up onto the porch for her. He sat Rachel's urn carefully beside the suitcase.

It was dark. Mrs. Brown hadn't left on the porch light.

"Are you going to be all right?" he asked gently, holding her by the shoulders.

"Yes. My head's fine, now. Stuart," she added slowly, "thank you, for all you've done."

"It was nothing," he replied. "If you hear from that drug-dealing boyfriend of Rachel's, you call me. Okay?"

She nodded. "I will."

"And if you remember anything about where that journal might be, call me."

"I'll do that."

He lifted his hand to her face and traced her soft cheek. "We didn't get to do anything about those jewels, but I promise you I'll get in touch with the man in a day or so and arrange to get them back to him. If you're sure that's what you want."

"It's what's right," she countered quietly. "Rachel had no scruples. I do."

He smiled. "Yes, I know."

She didn't want him to leave. She'd gotten used to being with him, almost intimately, in the past couple of days. Tonight she'd sleep alone. If her headache came back, she'd have to take aspirin and pray for sleep, because he wouldn't be there.

"Don't look like that, or I won't be able to leave you," he said suddenly, his jaw tautening. "I don't want to go home alone, either."

Her soft expulsion of breath was audible.

"Blind little woman," he whispered tenderly, and bent his head. He lifted her completely against his hard body while he kissed her. It took a long time, and when he finally let her down, she shivered with the overwhelming desire he'd kindled in her.

A sudden flash of lightning lit up the sky, followed by a crash of thunder. She jumped. "You be careful going home," she said firmly.

He smiled. "Wear a raincoat if it's still raining in the morning when you go to work," he countered.

She smiled back. Rain was blowing onto the porch, getting them both wet. Neither was wearing a raincoat.

"Go inside," he said, giving her a gentle push toward the door. "I'll phone you tomorrow."

"Okay. Good night."

"Sleep tight," he replied, and winked at her.

She watched him from the open door, after she'd put all her things inside, including the urn with Rachel's ashes. It was as if her life was just now beginning.

Mrs. Brown had gone to bed. Apparently, so had Lita. Ivy moved all her things into her room and placed Rachel's ashes on the mantel. The next day, she was going to see about having them interred in the cemetery next to their father.

She lay awake for a long time, thinking about her new relationship with Stuart. She hoped his attitude meant that they had a shared future ahead. She wished for it with all her heart.

The next day, she remembered that she'd put Rachel's diary in her purse. So before she started her rounds of clients, she took it out and read it. What she'd thought was an ordinary recitation of events turned out to be something quite different. There were names, phone numbers and other numbers that seemed more like map coordinates than anything else.

She read them over and over, and grew even more puzzled. Then she pulled out the letter Rachel had received from a San Antonio law firm. It was dynamite. The letter referenced certain materials she'd put in a safe-deposit box in Jacobsville, to be opened if anything unexpected happened to her. The attorneys wrote to remind her that she hadn't forwarded them the key.

She sat back with a harsh sigh. Rachel was involved in something illegal, she just knew it. And she was clearly blackmailing someone else. Was it the millionaire whose jewels she'd kept? Or was it her boyfriend? Or one of his clients?

Shc knew immediately that this was too big for her to handle. She phoned Sheriff Hayes Carson and had him come to the boardinghouse. She met him on the porch, smiling as she invited him into the house and into the kitchen, where she had coffee brewing.

"Thanks for coming so quickly," she said, sitting down after she'd poured coffee for them both. "I'm in over my head on this stuff. Here. See what you make of it."

She handed him the journal and the letter from the attorneys in San Antonio that she'd found in Rachel's apartment. He read them, frowning. "These are GPS coordinates," he remarked, running his finger along the columns in the diary. "I recognize two of the names, too," he added. His dark eyes met hers. "They're deep in the Mexican drug cartel that Cara Dominguez was running until her arrest. One of the Culebra drug cartel named here," he added, "is Julie Merrill. The other is Willie Carr, the baker you gave the message about flour to."

She grimaced. "Oh, boy."

"This information is worth its weight in gold, all by itself. But the key she mentioned is missing," he continued. "That key is dynamite. Your life could be in danger if any of her associates even think you might have it. We're talking multimillion dollar drug shipments here."

"But I don't know where the key is," she said miserably. "I looked through all the stuff I got from her apartment. I even checked the quilts to make sure she hadn't slipped it into the backing." She shook her head. "I can't imagine where she might have left it."

"Was there anything else that you took from the apartment?" he asked.

"Just the jewelry she was hoarding," she said miserably. "From that elderly millionaire she was involved with. Stuart and I put them in a safe-deposit box in New York City, under his name. He's arranging to get them back to the man."

He frowned. "Was there a locket, or any sort of thing a key could be hidden in?"

"No," she assured him.

He sipped coffee, frowning. "I don't want to spook you, but isn't there someone you could move in with until we find that key?"

She would have said Stuart and Merrie only a day before. But Stuart hadn't called her, as he'd promised he would. She hadn't heard from Merrie, either. She couldn't just invite herself to be a houseguest under the circumstances.

"No," she said sadly.

"Okay," he said with resolution. "I want to know where you are day and night for the next few days. I'm going to get in touch with Alexander Cobb at DEA and talk to our police chief, Cash Grier, as well. We'll arrange to keep you under surveillance." He picked up the padded diary. "Will you trust me with this?" he asked.

"Of course."

His thumb smoothed over the back of it. Suddenly he went still. His eyes went to the diary. He put it on the table and pulled out his pocketknife. Before she could ask what he was doing, he opened the diary with the pages down on the table and slit the fabric of the back. Seconds later, he pulled out a safe-deposit box key.

"Good heavens!" she exclaimed. "How did you . . . ?"

"Sheer luck," he said. "I felt it under my thumb. I'll have to contact those attorneys in San Antonio and see what the key fits. I may need you, as next of kin, to authorize me to access it."

"Before I can do that, I'll need to meet with Blake

160

Kemp," she replied, "and see about the paperwork to get Rachel's estate—such as it is—into probate."

"If you're not busy right now, I'll drive you over there," he said. "I'd like to talk to him as well."

She grinned. "That would be terrific. Thanks."

Hayes went out onto the porch while she phoned Blake Kemp's office and found him free if they could make it there within the half hour. She assured his new secretary—he'd only recently married his old secretary Violet and they were expecting a child—that she and Hayes would be right over.

She climbed into the unmarked sheriff's car with Hayes, cradling the diary and the attorney's letter with her purse on her lap.

As they pulled out of the driveway, a car that had been sitting parked by the side of the road was quickly started. It pulled onto the road, following slowly behind Hayes Carson's car.

Hayes sat in the waiting room while Ivy spoke to Blake Kemp about Rachel's estate. She didn't have bank statements or any documentation about her possessions, but the attorney's letter intimated that they did. He read the letter, frowning.

Blake shook his head. "She was nothing like you," he said quietly.

"She told Dad that I wasn't his," she replied. "Is there a way to find out . . . ?"

"Not his?" he exclaimed. His blue eyes darkened. "For God's sake, your mother would never have cheated on your father! She worshipped him, despite his bad temper and the way he knocked her around. Besides all that, he'd have killed any man who touched her!"

"Are you sure?" she asked, relieved.

"Yes, I am," he said flatly. "Rachel got exactly what she deserved, Ivy. She was a horror of a human being. Why in God's name would she tell a lie like that?"

"Can't you guess? I can. She wanted everything Dad had when he died. If he thought I wasn't his blood daughter, why would he want to leave me anything?" she asked sadly.

"How many lives did that woman shatter?" he wondered aloud.

"Quite a few, I expect. Her boyfriend was trying to find the journal she kept. He was frantic about it," she recalled, "but it turned out to be her diary. I gave it to Hayes," she added. "He says it has some vital information about drug smuggling, of all things."

"There's one more thing about Rachel I don't imagine you know," he began, his face solemn. "She didn't just use drugs, Ivy. She sold them, beginning when she was a senior in high school. She always had a direct pipeline to the local drug trade. If she has the documentation mentioned in this letter, it probably names names. That would give Cash Grier a heads-up while he's trying to shut down the newest drug cartel members locally."

"That's what Hayes said," she replied with a smile. "He thinks it may show the position of some drug caches."

"I hope it does," he said. "This little community has gone through some hard times because of drug smuggling. I'd love to see the suppliers shut down."

"So would I."

"Don't worry about the rest of this," he told her. "I'll handle it. But I should talk to Stuart York about that jewelry."

"Yes," she said, concerned that he hadn't phoned her yet. She had her cell phone turned on and she'd been checking it all morning to make sure it was working. It was.

"Let's call Hayes in." He touched the intercom button and had the receptionist send Hayes down the hall to his office.

Hayes showed him the journal. It really was dynamite. It would be wonderful, Ivy thought, if they could really use it to shut down the drug dealers.

"Rachel's boyfriend knows this journal exists," Hayes said somberly. "I wouldn't put it past him to come down here if he thinks Ivy might have it. If Rachel gave her attorneys something damaging about him, and he knows it, he won't have a lot to lose. No evidence, no case."

Both men looked at Ivy.

"I can buy a gun," she began.

"No, you can't," Hayes said firmly. "I have an idea, about where you could stay."

"I can get a motel room . . ."

"You aren't thinking of Minette and her brood?" Blake asked hesitantly.

Hayes's face went taut. "She lives out of town, where anybody coming to the house would be immediately visible, and her ranch manager was a Secret Service agent some years ago."

"But Merrie York is your best friend," Blake interrupted, eyeing Ivy. "Surely you could stay with her. Stuart has an ex-fed working for him, too."

Her face colored. "Merrie lives in San Antonio," she said. "And I don't think Stuart's home . . ."

"Sure he's home," Hayes returned. "I saw him driving by this morning with that debutante from Houston he's been seeing."

Ivy felt the life drain out of her. The words kept repeating in her head. Stuart had held her and kissed her and treated her with such tenderness that she thought they were going to be together for life. Instead, the minute they got home from New York, he made a beeline for his latest conquest. He probably hadn't given Ivy a second thought. Maybe he even thought of the way he'd taken care of her as an act of mercy.

She closed her eyes. Pain echoed through her nerves.

"Are you all right?" Hayes asked, concerned. They had left the office and were now in the car.

She forced a smile. "I'm fine. Tell me about this Minette."

He seemed reluctant. "She owns the Jacobsville newspaper. You know that."

"But I've never met her," she pointed out.

He shrugged. "She lives with her aunt and two siblings, a half brother and a half sister. She's off today because there was a fire in the office and they had to call in a cleaning crew to pick up the mess and deal with the fire damage."

"Was it an accidental fire?" she asked.

"I don't know. She's been running some articles about the drug trade. I warned her that her new ace reporter was going to bring down some heat on the paper, but she wouldn't listen. The eager-beaver reporter is fresh out of journalism school looking for his first shrunken head to flaunt."

"If he points a finger at the wrong people, he'll get her sued."

"Been there, done that," he murmured. "She got Kemp to represent her and won the suit. But she's letting the kid push the wrong people. Sooner or later, there's going to be a tragedy. I tell her so, but she won't listen."

"She's a crusader," she mused.

He gave her a tight glare. "She's showing me that she doesn't take advice if it comes from my general direction. It may get her killed, in the end."

"You should find her some protection," she pointed out. "If she's trying to shut down the drug lords, you and Cash Grier might thank her for the help."

"You don't understand," he growled. "She isn't doing any of us any good. She's pointing out possible hiding places for the influx of illegal drugs and hammering home that foreign nationals are financing the traffic."

"They are."

"Ivy," he said heavily, "at the same time she's hammering the drug trade, she's holding out olive branches to illegal immigrants. She's making enemies on both sides of the drug issue."

Ivy's face softened. "You know Mario Xicara, don't you?"

He slowed for a turn. His lips thinned. "Yes."

"And his wife, Dolores, and their four little kids?"

"I know the family."

"In the village they came from in Guatemala, one man turned in a drug dealer and his whole family was gunned down. To punctuate the threat, they killed six other families as well. Mario escaped with his wife and children, but his parents and grandparents were among the dead, along with their new baby who was in the house when the drug dealer's minions came in firing."

"I know that, but . . ."

"They're applying for citizenship," she continued. "But now they have to be sent back to Guatemala until they can get temporary papers. The drug dealers are still around their village."

He grimaced. "There are always two sides to every issue," he reminded her.

"I know." She smiled. "But people are more than statistics."

He gave a turn signal. "I'll talk to Homeland Security. I know a man who works in ICE," he said with resignation, naming the enforcement arm of the immigration service.

"Thanks, Hayes."

"Any other small favors I can do you?" he teased.

"I'll make a list. Hayes, this isn't the way to my boardinghouse," she announced suddenly, as she realized they were heading out of town in the wrong direction.

"I know. I've got an idea."

CHAPTER TEN

MINETTE RAYNOR was twenty-four. She was managing editor of the weekly *Jacobsville Times*, the newspaper of Jacobs County. Her mother had inherited the paper from Minette's grandfather, and she ran it until her death. After that, her father and stepmother ran it. He'd died three years previously. Minette had grown up knowing how to sell ads, write copy, set type and paste up copy in the composing room. It was easy for her to step into her parents' shoes and run the paper. She was tall, slender, dark-eyed and blond, with a scattering of freckles over her nose. Her hair was her most incredible asset. It looked like a thick flow of pale gold that inched down her back almost to her waist. It was much longer than Ivy's.

From a deceased uncle, she'd inherited a ranch that raised steers for beef, and it was ramrodded by her late father's wrangler and two part-time cowboys who were students at the local community college. Her great-aunt Sarah lived with her and helped take care of Minette's half brother, Shane, who was eleven, and her half sister Julie, who was five. Minette's mother had died when she was ten, and her father had married Dawn Jenkies, a quiet librarian who adored him and Minette. Over their years together, she presented Dane with a son and a daughter, upon whom Minette doted. When Dawn died, and her father soon after of a heart attack, Minette was left to raise the children. It seemed to be a labor of love.

Hayes pulled up at her front steps, where she and the children were wielding paintbrushes, touching up the fading white of the door facing and wood trim. Minette, in jeans and a sweatshirt, got up, glaring at Hayes.

He glared back. "I need to ask a favor."

She looked furious. "I don't owe you any favors, Sheriff Carson," she said icily.

"I know that. But I have to put Ivy someplace where she'll be safe. Drug dealers may be after her."

Minette's eyes narrowed. She seemed to be biting her tongue.

Carson just looked uncomfortable. "The county will pay for her upkeep," he said curtly. "It's only for a few days."

Minette looked worriedly at her siblings.

"I'm going to have one of my deputies stay here, too," he added. "If you don't mind."

"I always wanted to open a hotel," Minette told him irritably. But when she saw Ivy's consternation, she went to her and smiled. "I'm sorry. You may have noticed that the sheriff and I don't get along. But you're welcome to stay. Aunt Sarah would love the company. I'm at work most days until late." She looked at Hayes viciously. "When I'm not overdosing men, that is."

"Cut it out," he bit off, avoiding her eyes.

Ivy knew at once that Merrie York was out of luck where Hayes was concerned. Something powerful was at work between these two. And it wasn't business.

The little girl, Julie, walked over to Hayes and looked up at him. "Do you got any little kids?" she asked softly.

"Careful, baby," Minette said softly, eyeing Hayes. "Rattlesnakes bite."

He glared at her. She glared back.

He looked down at Julie, who was blond like her half sister. "No, I don't have any kids," he said a little stiffly.

The child cocked her head at him. "That's very sad," she replied, sounding very grown up. "My sister says little kids are sweet." She frowned. "You don't look like a rattlesnake."

"Julie, would you get me a rag from the kitchen, please?" Minette asked her.

"Okay, Minette!" She ran up the steps and into the house.

"You're very welcome to stay with us," Minette told Ivy, her smile welcoming.

"I'll run you back to the boardinghouse to pack a bag," Hayes said.

Ivy hesitated. "Listen, are you sure this is necessary?"

"Mrs. Brown isn't going to be much protection if Rachel's boyfriend comes looking for you," he said.

She grimaced. "All right, then." She smiled at Minette. "I can cook," she said. "If you need help in the kitchen."

The other woman laughed. "Always. Aunt Sarah and I share kitchen duty, but neither of us is overly skilled. Still, we haven't poisoned anyone."

"Yet," Hayes enunciated coldly.

She stood up, eyes blazing. "Someday," she said slowly, "the truth is going to bite you in the neck! I didn't kill your brother. He killed himself. That's what you can't accept, isn't it, Hayes? You want a scape-goat . . . !"

"You bought the drug for him that he overdosed on!" Hayes shot back.

Minette stood erect, her face pale. "For the twentieth time, I never used drugs, or got drunk, or put a foot out of line in my life," she said proudly. "So how exactly do you think I'd know where to find illegal drugs in this town?"

He looked odd.

"Never mind," she continued. "I'm tired of beating a dead horse. Ivy, we'll get a room ready for you. The one thing we do have plenty of in this white elephant," she indicated the two-story Victorian house, "is room."

"Thanks," Ivy replied. "Hayes?"

He was staring at Minette, frowning. "What? Yes. We'll go now. Minette, I'd like to speak with Marsh."

"He's out in the barn, fixing a saddle."

Hayes took Ivy to the car, and he went to the barn. He was back in a couple of minutes. He got in the car and drove away.

Ivy didn't ask about his feud with the other woman, but she gathered that it had something to do with his brother's death. Everyone knew that Bobby Carson had died of a drug overdose three years earlier, just before Rachel went to New York. Why he thought Minette was responsible was curious. She was known locally for her hard stand on drug use and her support of antidrug programs in the schools.

"She's very nice," Ivy began.

Hayes didn't answer. "You'll be safe. Marsh will keep you safe. Nobody would think of looking for you out there, but even if they did, you'd see them coming a mile away. Not that I think the boyfriend will come all the way down here, since he isn't sure you've got that journal. But it's best to be cautious." He glanced at her. "I still think Merrie and Stuart would have let you stay with them."

She didn't answer him, either.

The next day, she authorized Hayes to open the safe-deposit box in the Jacobsville bank, with Police Chief Cash Grier and DEA Agent Alexander Cobb as witnesses. He picked her up and brought her to the bank.

It was a haul. Rachel had names, locations, dates, quantities of drugs shipped and the point of origin for a huge cocaine shipment. Implicated in the drug trafficking were her boyfriend, a local Jacobsville resident and two men who sat on Jacobsville's city council two years earlier.

"This is great." Cash Grier spoke for the other men as he read through the documentation. "This is enough evidence to shut down one of the biggest pipelines of illicit drugs in south Texas."

"We can certainly use it," Cobb agreed.

"Amen." Hayes smiled at Ivy. "Rachel made up for a lot with this," he said. "Regardless of her motive."

Ivy wondered about that motive. She didn't say it aloud, but she had a feeling that Rachel had been blackmailing somebody. She probably never expected to die, or to have played a big part in shutting down the drug trade in Jacobs County. It was the one noble act of Rachel's life.

It was decided that Ivy would stay at Minette's house. When she packed up her few things and told Mrs. Brown and Lita what was going on, they both tried to get her to stay.

"I have my father's old shotgun," Mrs. Brown said.

"I'm not afraid of drug dealers," Lita added.

"I know that, but it's going to take professionals to keep this from escalating," Ivy told them. "I don't want either of you in danger. Okay?"

They agreed, reluctantly.

Ivy left Rachel's ashes in her room for the time being. Once the fear of retribution from Rachel's boyfriend was past, she could take care of the funeral.

She was given a room next to Minette's, and she became part of the family overnight. Aunt Sarah, a tiny little woman with white hair, was a live wire. The children had sweet, loving natures. Minette had a wicked sense of humor.

"I'm surprised that Hayes would bring you here," she commented over steak and biscuits. "He really hates me."

"Maybe that's why," Ivy chuckled. "He seems to think I might be a target." She shook her head. "If anything happened to the kids," she added worriedly.

"Don't you worry," Minette assured her. "We have Marsh Bailey out in the bunkhouse. He was an IPSIC shooter. That's pistol competition," she clarified. "He worked for the U.S. Marshal's Service, and he never misses. God help the outlaw who shows up here uninvited."

"I hope he won't," Ivy said. "But Rachel's boyfriend has more to lose than most people. He might figure out that I have the journal she left, and come after me."

"I don't think he's that stupid," Minette ventured, sipping coffee. Her soft eyes pinned Ivy's across the supper table. "Think about it. There's a journal floating around that has names and addresses and the potential to explode the local drug trade. You don't know who's got it or where it is, but you know you'll get blamed if the authorities find it. Would you walk into the arena, or would you run for your life?"

Ivy felt better. "You know," she said, "I think I'd run."

Minette smiled. "I think I would, too."

For the next two days, Ivy stayed with the Raynors. She got her ledgers from the boardinghouse and drove her little VW back to Minette's house. Hayes came by to check on her and mentioned that they'd heard nothing from their informants about the New York connection to the drug trade. However, he did say that the baker had been arrested and charged with drug trafficking. Julie Merrill was still on the loose, however, and nobody, including her father, had any idea where she'd gone.

"We did phone the Brooklyn precinct that worked your sister's death," he added. "It seems that her boyfriend was involved in an accident yesterday. He's in the hospital and not expected to live."

"What happened to him?" she exclaimed.

"It seems he walked into an elevator shaft in his own apartment building," Hayes told her. "There were two eyewitnesses. They have mob ties, of course. The word on the street is that Smith was trying to trespass on another drug dealer's territory."

"Tough," Ivy said, without any real regret. The man who'd helped Rachel feed her habit had gone the same way she had. It was a fitting sort of end. She said so.

"I have to agree."

"Then, do you think I could go home?" she ventured.

He hesitated. "I can't stop you. Smith won't be a problem, but there are some shadowy members of the drug cartel still on the loose. You won't know who they are."

"I have an answer to that," she replied.

"What?"

"Let Minette do a story about the Jacobsville drug link and say that all Rachel's records are now in the hands of law enforcement," she suggested. "That should put a kink in their operation—and keep them out of Jacobsville."

He began to smile. "I like the way you think. Okay. I'll talk to her about it."

"And I can go home? I still have Rachel's funeral to arrange."

He nodded. "Go ahead. If you need me, you know where I am."

"Yes, I do. Thanks, Hayes."

"No problem."

She did go back to the boardinghouse, but she was nervous, even under the circumstances. She didn't want to endanger Mrs. Brown and Lita. On the other hand, she hadn't felt right about endangering Minette's young siblings. If only Stuart was still speaking to her. She agonized over his defection to the pretty debutante. He'd just dropped Ivy like a rock, and when she needed him most. If she only knew why!

The next day, she drove out to the cemetery, where the funeral home director and his assistant were waiting. The trees were all bare. It was a gray day. It was misting rain as well. It looked such a forlorn place with the cold wind whipping Ivy's hair around.

A small grave had been dug next to her father's, to

receive Rachel's urn. There wasn't anyone there except herself. She had thought of putting the obituary notice in the paper, but Rachel had left plenty of enemies in Jacobsville, and few friends.

She was wearing a long gray dress with an equally long tweed coat. The wind was crisp and cruel. She'd been awake half the night thinking about Stuart and wondering what she'd done to make him stay away. They'd been so close in New York. Now, he didn't seem to remember her at all. At least when he'd disliked her, she'd seen him from time to time. She ached to be with him. Even just the sight of him at a distance would feed her hungry heart. But apparently that wasn't going to happen.

The wind blew coldly around her as she stared at the bronze urn that contained the only human remains of her sister. She'd never felt so alone.

The funeral director's assistant, who was also a lay minister, said the words over Rachel's ashes. As Ivy listened, she was sorry that her sister's life had been so wasted, so full of selfish greed. If only Rachel had been different. If only she'd cared about Ivy. She closed her eyes as the prayer ended, hoping that it had helped the older woman in her path to the other side of life.

When she looked up, she was astonished, delighted, shocked to see Stuart York striding toward her. He wasn't smiling. His wide-brimmed dress hat was pulled down low over his eyes. He was dressed in city clothes, a gray suit that made him look distinguished.

He paused at the graveside and looked down at Ivy, who couldn't hide her delight, or her wounds.

"I'm sorry I'm late," he said curtly. "I couldn't find out what time you were having the service. If I'd known, Merrie would have come down, too."

"I didn't think anyone would come," she said simply.

His eyes narrowed. "You didn't think, period," he said shortly. His big hand caught her small one and held it tight. She looked up at him, feeling suddenly safe and confident, and tears misted her eyes.

The funeral home director gave Ivy his condolences, along with the lay minister, and then beckoned to the workman to put the urn in its resting place.

"Do you want to stay for this?" Stuart asked.

She nodded. "It's such a sad way to die," she said.

His hand tightened. He didn't say anything.

He walked with her to her vehicle, and his eyes said what he thought of it. "You'd be safer riding a one-wheeled bicycle," he said flatly.

"It doesn't look like much," she agreed, "but it does run. Mostly."

He turned her to him, taking her gently by the shoulders. "I saw you ride off with Hayes Carson the morning after we got in," he said coldly. "You were with him again the next day."

"Yes," she said, surprised, "because he and Chief Grier . . ."

". . . had to oversee the opening of the safe-deposit box," he finished for her, dark eyes flickering. "You could have called and told me that, Ivy."

"Yes?" Her own eyes began to glitter. "And you could have called me, instead of riding around town with your pretty debutante visitor!"

The hard look on his face melted. He began to smile. "Were you jealous?" he taunted softly.

"Were you?" she shot right back.

He laughed. It was a wicked sort of laugh.

It made her cheeks color. She lowered her eyes to his chest. "I thought you'd had second . . . I mean, I thought . . ."

He put his forefinger gently across her lips. "So did I," he whispered.

She met his eyes and couldn't look away. He bent and drew his lips tenderly across her soft mouth. She started to reach up, but he caught her arms and held them down.

"No," he whispered. "Not in a cemetery."

She cleared her throat. "You started it."

"And you have no willpower," he teased. "I love it."

She laughed shyly.

"Why did you go out to Mincttc Raynor's house with Hayes?"

"How did you . . . ?"

"Two thousand pairs of curious eyes live in this town," he said with affection. "The druggist and the clerk at the bank mentioned it, even before Cash Grier told me the whole story. Which you could have done," he added shortly.

She started to argue, but she realized that he was right. She moved restlessly and didn't look at him.

"My pride was hurt, when I heard about you riding around with that woman."

"She was visiting her uncle. I'm doing a business deal with him. She needed a ride to town, and I obliged." He tilted her chin up. "Which I could have let Chayce do. But I'd seen you with Hayes and I figured somebody would see me with her. In fact," he added wickedly, "I drove right by Hayes Carson's office with her. He saw us."

"Rachel gave us enough information to hang the local drug lords out to dry," she said. "Maybe, in one way, she redeemed herself. How about the jewelry?" she added.

"I flew up there yesterday and had the millionaire's attorney meet me at the bank," he told her. "He was astonished that you'd want to give him back what amounted to a king's ransom. He wants to give you a reward."

"I wouldn't take one," she said.

He smiled. "I told him that. Know what he said?"

"What?"

"That you were one in a million, and I was a very lucky man."

"You weren't thinking that, I bet."

"Not at the time, no." He frowned. "You haven't said why you went to Minette's with Hayes. He hates her. Everybody knows he thinks she gave his brother the drugs that killed him."

"He said that Marsh would watch out for me, and that the place was situated so that you could see someone coming two miles away. There's no way to sneak up on it."

"He's right, there—Marsh was a federal agent. But so was Chayce, who works for me. You'll be safer at my house."

"Are you sure about that?"

He grimaced and took a long breath. "I asked Merrie if she could take a few days off and come home to chaperone me with a woman. She laughed her head off when I had to admit that it was you."

"She would."

He brought her hand to his mouth and kissed the palm. "I'll follow you to your boardinghouse. You can leave your car there and come with me in mine."

She hesitated. "I've only just come home from Minette's place, and I've been worried about my boardinghouse friends. Rachel's boyfriend is on his way out of the world," she added, pausing to explain what had happened. "But it's still possible that one of the cartel people could come looking for me. If they see my car there, it might put Mrs. Brown and Lita in danger," she cautioned.

"Suppose we leave it at Hayes's office?"

"Would he mind?"

"Hell, no. Hayes only lives for the adrenaline rushes his job gives him. That's why he's never married. No woman in her right mind would marry him."

"He and Minette are like flint and steel together," she commented.

"Yes, I know," he replied. "One day, there's going to

be a fearful explosion between them, and anything could happen. That's why I've discouraged Merrie."

"Merrie isn't stupid, you know," she said gently.

"Well, not in most ways. Come on. Let's go."

Life was sweet again. Ivy forgot the cartel, Rachel's burial, everything as she and Stuart dropped her car off at the sheriff's office.

"I wondered why she wasn't staying with you," Hayes commented to Stuart. "She and Merrie have been friends forever."

"We had a misunderstanding," Stuart replied. He caught Ivy's hand in his, to make the point, just in case Hayes had missed it. "But we've cleared things up. Merrie's coming home for a few days, too. Chayce and I, and the boys, will make sure Ivy's safe."

Hayes grinned wickedly. "What about the pretty debutante?"

Stuart raised an eyebrow. "Her fiancé is waiting for her back in Houston."

"Oh," Hayes remarked, with a speculative look at Ivy, who flushed.

"Thanks for letting me keep my car here," Ivy said. "I was worried about leaving it at my boardinghouse."

"No problem," Hayes said. "It might work to our advantage if they think you're staying here in my office." He grinned. "In fact, I hope they do think it. I'll call Cash and tell him, too."

"Let me know if you catch anyone," Ivy asked.

"Of course."

· · ·

"Will he really call me, do you think, if he catches somebody?" Ivy asked as they drove to Stuart's house.

"I imagine so. You're involved, whether you want to be or not." He took her hand in his and held it tightly. "I found out something else in New York that I didn't share with Hayes."

"What?" she asked, certain that it was something unpleasant.

"The millionaire was concerned enough to hire a private detective. He shadowed Rachel before she took the overdose. She led him to one of the bigger names in drug distribution in the country. The detective said that she was blackmailing the man with information she'd gleaned from her boyfriend. She'd hidden the evidence, and nobody could find out where."

"Did they kill her?" she asked worriedly.

"It wouldn't have been wise to do that, considering that they didn't know exactly what she had on them, or where it was kept."

"She'd used drugs for years," she argued. "She wouldn't have taken an overdose deliberately."

"There were no signs of force on her body," he replied. "I checked with the medical examiner."

"Then, how . . . ?"

"They did a toxicology screen, though," he added. "The stuff she injected was a hundred percent pure. She used too much."

"Did she have help using too much?" she asked warily.

"Her boyfriend was right in the middle of her

schemes," he said. "It's possible that he deliberately gave her the pure drug, instead of the drug that had been cut, to save himself. He might not have known about the evidence she had. He might have thought she was bluffing. She would have used her regular dose, which was fatal because of the substitution. It would still look like suicide."

"Tough luck for him, if it's true," she said curtly. "Because when the drug pipeline gets shut down by the DEA, they're going to want to punish someone, and he's the only one left alive that they can get to. If he lives, he may wish he'd died."

"Yes." He glanced at her. "Poetic justice, you might say."

She had to agree that it was. "Poor Rachel," she said, shaking her head. "She was always greedy."

"Always." He squeezed her hand. "She was at that party with Hayes's brother Bobby, you know," he added. "She knew the dealers and where to get the drugs, and she had a case on Bobby at the time because he was rich. She might have thought she was doing him a favor, so when it went bad, she put it around that Minette did the dirty work."

"That would be like her," she agreed. "But Hayes still thinks Minette did it."

"God knows why," he said. "Minette sings in the choir at church, teaches a Sunday school class and she's never had so much as a speeding ticket. She never even knew any kids who were on the wrong side of the law."

"Hayes is blind when it comes to her," she said.

He smiled. "Men tend to be that way when they're afraid of being caught," he told her. "Freedom becomes a religion when you're over thirty."

"I guess most men don't want to settle down."

"Oh, we do, eventually. Especially when we realize that some other man might be poaching on our territory." He glanced at her. "I was ready to punch Hayes."

She felt her cheeks go hot. She smiled. "Were you?"

"Are you sure there's nothing between you?" he persisted.

"I'm very sure," she replied, linking her fingers closer into his.

He smiled.

Merrie was already at the house when they got there, to Ivy's faint disappointment. She'd hoped to have some time alone with Stuart.

He got out and opened her door, helping her out. He led her up the steps, leaving the car in the driveway.

"I didn't believe him when he told me," Merrie teased, hugging her friend.

"I still can't," Ivy confessed, with a shy glance at Stuart.

"Come on in," Merrie said. "Mrs. Rhodes has already made some tea cakes and coffee for us."

"I'd love something hot to drink," Ivy replied. "It was cold at the cemetery."

"I would have been there, too, if I'd known," Merrie said gently. "I just got here about twenty minutes ago. I'm sorry about Rachel."

"Me, too," Ivy replied. "I wish she'd made better choices in her life."

"I hope that information she furnished helps close doors around here for the drug trade," Stuart said as he sat beside Ivy on the sofa. "It's more dangerous than ever when you have two factions fighting for supremacy."

"Rachel actually turned informant?" Merrie exclaimed.

"She did," Ivy replied, and told her the whole story, interrupted briefly by Mrs. Rhodes bearing a silver tray with coffee and tea cakes, milk and sugar and china.

"But why did Hayes take you to Minette's house?" Merrie asked curiously. "He hates her."

"I wouldn't take any bets on that," Stuart replied, munching on a tea cake.

"They're very explosive together," Ivy said warily.

Merrie sighed. "I had a feeling about that," she confessed. She grinned. "I had a real crush on Hayes when I was about sixteen, but I'm not stupid enough to think we'd do well as a couple. We're too different. Besides," she confessed with a shy smile, "there's a very handsome divorced doctor I work with at the hospital."

"Tell me all about him," Ivy coaxed.

Stuart finished his coffee and stood up. "I'll pass," he said with a grin. "I have things to do. Don't go away," he told Ivy.

"I won't," she promised.

He winked at her, leaving her flushed and delighted.

"I still can't believe it!" Merrie exclaimed when he'd

gone out of earshot. "You and my brother! I thought you hated each other!"

"So did I," Ivy confessed. "I've loved him since I was eighteen."

"I think he feels something similar. He was livid about seeing you around town with Hayes. No man gets that mad about a woman he hates." She laughed. "You can't imagine how relieved I was! I was sure you were falling for Hayes, and I knew that he and Minette were passionate about hating each other. One day, mark my words, there's going to be an explosion between the two of them. I didn't want you to be hurt," she added gently.

Ivy felt the relief all the way to her toes. She just smiled. "Thanks. But I wasn't kidding when I said Hayes was a friend. I've loved Stuart forever, it seems. I can't believe he feels the same."

Merrie chuckled. "I can."

Ivy leaned forward. "Well, now that we've got Hayes out of the way, tell me about this sexy doctor you work with!"

After supper, Merrie discreetly went upstairs to watch a movie on pay-per-view with Mrs. Rhodes while Stuart went into his study with Ivy and closed the door. As an afterthought, he locked it behind him.

Ivy was nervous and delighted, all at once, as he drew her into his arms.

"I'm starving," he whispered as his mouth covered hers.

She realized quickly that he wasn't talking about food. She held on for dear life and kissed him back with her whole heart. She felt him lift her, carry her, to the long leather sofa. He put her down on it and joined her, drawing her completely against his powerful body.

She shivered at the sensations that rose like a flood, almost searing her as passion consumed them both.

He ground her hips into his, groaning when she jerked and gasped into his demanding mouth. She made no protest at all when she felt his lean hands go under her blouse, against her bare skin.

"Your body is softer than silk," he breathed into her mouth. "Warm and sweet to touch. I want you, Ivy."

She wanted him, too, but they were getting in over their heads and she was an old-fashioned woman. She grew more nervous as his ardor increased. Helpless, she stiffened.

He hesitated, lifting his head to look down into her wide, apprehensive eyes. His own narrowed. "Yes," he whispered. "You want me. You'd give in, if I asked you to. But you don't want it to happen like this, do you?"

She swallowed, knowing she might lose him forever if she told the truth. "I . . . I was raised to believe that some things are still wrong even if the whole world says they're right."

She looked up at him nervously, waiting for him to get up and walk out, or just to make some sarcastic comment. He was a worldly man in his thirties. He'd said he wasn't a marrying man, and she wasn't capable of sleeping with him out of wedlock. Her heart fell to her knees. She couldn't go on living if she lost him, now. What would she do? Her eyes pleaded with his as the silence grew around them. It was, truly, the moment of truth.

CHAPTER ELEVEN

AND then, when Ivy was certain she'd lost, Stuart began to smile. It wasn't a sarcastic smile, either. He rolled over onto his side and traced patterns on her soft, swollen mouth. His shirt was open and her fingers were tangled in the thick hair that covered his chest. She didn't remember unfastening buttons, but she must have. Her own blouse and bra were down around her waist.

"I told you, I don't seduce virgins," he whispered deeply.

"I remember," she whispered back.

"I do, however, marry them," he murmured against her lips.

Her eyes widened. "You want to . . . to marry mc?"

He kissed her eyelids closed. "Of course I do," he replied huskily. "I wanted you when you were just eighteen. I've gone almost out of my mind wanting you since then, and hating myself for it. You're so young, Ivy," he told her, hugging her close. "But I can't live without you."

She clung to him, burying her face in his warm throat. "I can't live without you, either, Stuart," she confessed on a broken sob. "I love you . . . !"

His mouth stopped the words. He kissed her until her mouth was sore and they were both on the verge of surrender.

Whether it was by accident or by design, a loud knock at the door announced Merrie.

"Who wants cake and ice cream?" she called.

Stuart laughed. "Both of us!" he called back, winking at Ivy, who was delightfully flushed.

"Coming right up. You two coming out to get it?"

Stuart made a face. "Sure," he replied.

"Okay! Five minutes!"

Her footsteps died away.

Stuart's eyes began to glitter wickedly as he eased Ivy onto her back and slid over her. "Five whole minutes," he murmured against her soft mouth. "Let's make the best of them, sweetheart."

They did, too.

Amid plans for a big, society wedding that Ivy really didn't want, Chief Cash Grier and Sheriff Hayes Carson came to talk to Ivy. Stuart had gone out onto the ranch because there was a problem with some equipment, and Merrie was in town ordering invitations and a wedding cake.

Mrs. Rhodes led them into the living room, where Ivy was making a list of people she wanted to invite to the wedding.

"What can I do for you?" she asked them, smiling as she offered them chairs around the big, open fireplace that was blazing, cozy and warm in the large room.

"We thought you might like to know how things are going since we got Rachel's packet of information," Hayes told her.

"Would I ever!" she replied.

"It turns out that her boyfriend's main supplier was from Jacobsville," Cash Grier said. "Do you remember back last year when two of my patrol officers arrested a drunk politician and his daughter slandered me in the press?"

"Everybody remembers that," she said.

"Well, his daughter, Julie Merrill, was up to her neck in drug trafficking, along with the two commissioners who resigned from the city council and vanished."

"Julie was arrested and accused of arson for trying to burn down Libby Collins's house, wasn't she?" she replied. "And then she skipped bond and vanished, about the same time that Dominguez woman took over Manuel Lopez's old drug territory."

"Good memory, Ivy," Hayes chuckled.

"Better than mine," Cash agreed, grinning. "Anyway, we couldn't find her anyplace and, believe me, we looked. So this information Rachel left pointed to a hotel in downtown San Antonio where one of her drug-dealing boyfriend's contacts lived. Guess who the contact turned out to be?"

"Julie Merrill?!"

"The very same," Cash told her. "We've got her in custody. She's lodged in the county jail awaiting arraignment."

"Will that shut down the drug trade locally?" Ivy

asked. "And what about those two councilmen?"

"They're still hiding out somewhere," Hayes drawled. "But we'll turn them up sooner or later. Meanwhile, Dominguez has a successor."

"Do you know who it is?" she asked.

Cash and Hayes glanced at each other and some silent message passed between them. "We have an idea," Cash said. "We're working on proof. One of Cy Parks's old friends is going to help us out. He's a Mexican national with some long-held grudges."

"Rodrigo Ramirez," Ivy murmured thoughtfully.

"How do you know about him?" Cash asked suspiciously.

"I know Colby Lane's new wife, Sarina," she said. "She mentioned that Colby and Rodrigo had some, shall we say, problems during the time they were working on breaking the Dominguez case."

"Translated," Hayes said with a droll smile at Cash, "that means that Colby and Rodrigo could hardly stay in the same room together without exchanging threats of violence."

"Well, Rodrigo and Sarina had been partners for three years, after all," Cash pointed out.

"Yes, well, Colby and Sarina had been married and had a child together. Anyway," Hayes continued, "we have a lead on where Dominguez's lieutenant, who's taking over the Culebra cartel, is hiding out. Rodrigo's going to infiltrate it."

"What's Sarina going to say to that?" Ivy asked. "She and Rodrigo worked together busting up Dominguez's operation. Sarina's DEA, too, you know."

Cash chuckled. "Cobb doesn't want to let her resign. He says she can go undercover as Rodrigo's contact. Colby wants her to work for me. So do I," he added. "I only have one investigator, and it's a big county. I was hoping that she'd start right away. But Cobb offered her this peach of a case and she walked right over Colby and took it."

"Colby's really crazy about her," Ivy mentioned.

"Yes, and vice versa," Cash said. He sighed. "Well, maybe one day Colby will find a way to convince her to resign. Meanwhile, he and Bernadette hold down the fort on their ranch in Jacobsville while Sarina works nights."

"Is he still teaching tactics for Eb Scott?" she asked.

They nodded. "There was one other confession in Rachel's papers," Cash added slowly. "We thought you ought to know. She admitted that she gave Bobby Carson the drug that killed him."

Ivy's gasp was audible. She glanced at Hayes, whose face was as closed as a clam shell. "She confessed? But why?"

"Who knows?" Cash replied. "Maybe she had a premonition. Whatever her reason, she made amends for a lot of bad things she'd done in her life."

"Was there anything about me?" Ivy wanted to know. She hadn't even asked to read the papers, certain that they were all about drug trafficking and not about personal matters.

Cash hesitated.

"No," Hayes replied quietly. "She just noted that she guessed all her things would go to her sister at her death. It wasn't a will. She wasn't planning to die. But she knew that blackmailing drug lords is an iffy business. I guess she wanted to make the point."

Ivy felt her heart sink. She'd hoped for more than that.

"Don't lie to her," Cash said coldly. "Telling the truth is always the best way, even if it seems brutal." He looked at Ivy. "She said she'd told her boyfriend that you'd have all the blackmail information in case something happened to her."

"Dear God!" Ivy exclaimed, feeling sick.

"That wasn't necessary," Hayes said curtly.

"It was," Cash disagreed. "Mean people don't usually change, Ivy," he added. "If anything, they get meaner. She put you in the line of fire deliberately by telling Jerry Smith she'd given you the evidence."

"I'm not surprised," she said sadly. "She always hated me, from the time I was old enough to know who she was. My life was hell when I was a child."

Hayes pursed his lips. "Not anymore," he mused. "I noticed that Merrie York was at the engravers ordering wedding invitations this morning for you and Stuart."

She burst out laughing. "There's no such thing as a secret in Jacobsville."

"Damned straight," Cash agreed. "Are we getting invited?"

"Everybody's getting invited," Ivy replied with a

smile. "I would have liked to elope, but Stuart says we're going to have all the trimmings."

"I love weddings," Hayes said. "It's the only time I get decent cake."

"No fair," Ivy protested. "Barbara makes wonderful cakes at her café."

"I eat on the run, mostly," Hayes said.

"Are Jerry's friends going to come after me, when they know about Rachel's confession?" she worried.

"Not likely," Cash said with a grin. "Jerry survived his fall, against all the odds, and he's turning state's evidence. He pointed out his management-level supplier, who was picked up in New York City this morning and charged with drug trafficking. It seems this supplier had enough methamphetamine and crack cocaine in a rented, vacant apartment to qualify him for superdealer status. Federal charges," he continued, "and they carry long prison sentences. Cobb and the DEA had already picked up the ex-state senator's daughter in San Antonio, and we hear that the two ex-councilmen implicated in the scheme are trying to make it to Mexico."

"If they do, Rodrigo will push them back across the border and yell for the police," Hayes chuckled.

"I'm just glad it's over," Ivy said quietly. "It's been a long week."

"It certainly has," Hayes agreed.

Ivy wondered how he'd taken the news that Minette had never given his little brother the drugs that cost him his life. He might not believe it just yet. His vendetta against the woman had gone on for some time. Maybe he liked hating her.

They left a few minutes later, and she went back to her list.

The wedding, predictably, was the social event of the season. The church was decorated in white and red poinsettias, because it was only a few weeks before Christmas. Ivy wore a white gown with a train and a trailing veil that Stuart had bought for her at Neiman Marcus. She looked in the mirror and couldn't believe that this was her. She'd never dreamed that Stuart would want to marry her one day, when she was cocooned in her daydreams. She smiled at her reflection, flushing a little with happiness.

She walked down the aisle alone. She'd had offers from townspeople to give her away, but it seemed right to make the walk all by herself. You couldn't really give people away in these enlightened times, she'd told Stuart. If anything, she was giving herself.

Stuart stood at the beautiful arbor of poinsettias where the minister was waiting. He looked down the aisle as Ivy walked toward him and the look on his face was fascinating to her. This worldly, experienced man looked very much like a young boy on his first date. His eyes were eloquent.

She stopped beside him with her bouquet of white roses and lily of the valley and faced him shyly, with her veil draped delicately over her face, while the minister read the vows.

Finally the ring was on her finger, and on his. He lifted the beautiful lacy veil to look upon her for the first time as a bride.

"Beautiful," he whispered, as he bent to kiss her with exquisite tenderness. "Mrs. York," he added, smiling.

She beamed. She could have walked on air. She was the happiest woman in Texas, and she looked it.

Everyone in town was there. The big families, the little families, friends and acquaintances filled the church and flowed out into the yard.

"At least," she whispered to him at the reception, "nobody started a mixer, like they did at Blake Kemp's wedding to his Violet."

"It's early, yet," he cautioned, nodding toward a fuming Minette Raynor glaring up at a taciturn Hayes Carson.

"He doesn't believe she wasn't responsible, does he?" she mused.

"He doesn't want to believe it," he corrected. "Here, precious, take a bite of the cake so the photographer can make us immortal."

She flushed at the endearment and nibbled the white cake as the flash enveloped them. The camera captured similar exquisite moments until the happy couple finally climbed into a waiting white limousine and sped away toward the airport.

Jamaica, Ivy thought as she lay exhausted in Stuart's strong arms, was a dreamy place for a honeymoon. Not that they'd seen much of it yet. The minute the bellboy had deposited their luggage, received his tip and left the room, they'd ended up in the bed.

Ivy knew the mechanics of it, from her romantic novels and blunt articles in women's magazines. But reading about it and doing it were two very different things.

The sensations Stuart drew from her untried body were so powerful that they frightened her. She lost control of herself almost at once. His mouth and his hands coaxed a response out of her that would make her blush afterward. He teased her, encouraged her, praised her as he drew her with him from one peak to an even higher one.

There was one tiny flash of pain, and then nothing except sheer heat and passion that built on itself until she was shivering, exploding with pleasure, begging for relief from the tension that pulled her poor body so taut that it felt likely to explode.

And it did, in a maelstrom of excited delight that was beyond rational description. She cried out endlessly as her body arched up to receive his in helpless trembling thrusts.

He found his own relief just as she did, and then collapsed over her. She cradled him in her arms, drunk on ecstasy, blind with satiation.

After a few breathless minutes, he managed to lift his head and look down into her misty, happy eyes.

"Now I know you're disappointed," he said dryly, "that we rushed it like this. But later, I promise, I'll torture you with passion and make you scream like a wildcat when I satisfy you."

"Dis . . . appointed?" she asked, blank-eyed.

He pursed his lips. "You're not disappointed?"

"Good Lord, Stuart!" she exclaimed, barely able to breathe even now. "I thought I was going to die!"

He chuckled. "I must be better than I thought I was," he told her. He bent and kissed her eyelids. "I wanted to go slow, but I just lost it. I've waited so long for you, little one. Years and years. For the past year or so," he added huskily, "I've been as celibate as a man stranded on a desert island. I wasn't able to want anyone but you. So I couldn't draw it out the way I meant to, tonight."

She was delighted with the confession. Her long legs curled around his and her eyes half-closed in satisfaction. If she were a cat, she mused, she'd be purring. "I don't have a single complaint."

"It didn't hurt?" he persisted.

"Only a little. Mostly, I was too busy to notice."

He nibbled her lower lip. "I'm good," he drawled.

She grinned and punched him in the ribs. "Very good. I think. My memory seems to be slipping." She glanced up at him, drawing her fingers through the thick hair on his chest. "Could you do all that again, do you think, so I can make up my mind?"

"Darlin'," he whispered into her parting lips, "I would be delighted . . . !"

The next day, holding hands and walking along the beach while the waves crashed on the sand beside them, she wondered if anyone had ever been as happy as she was right now.

She leaned her head against his bare shoulder and kissed it. "Did I mention that I loved you?" she asked softly.

"I believe you did," he replied, and pulled her close. He looked down into her wide, radiant eyes. "But I didn't." He traced a path down her soft cheek, and his eyes were solemn. "I could have told you anytime in the past two years that I loved you. I still do. I always will."

It was powerful, hearing the words. She could hardly breathe. "Really?"

"Really." He bent and kissed her eyelids closed. "We've had a nice breakfast and some comfortable exercise. What would you like to do next, Mrs. York?"

She grinned wickedly, tugged his head down and whispered in his ear.

His eyebrows arched. "Do you know, that's exactly what I'd like to do next, too!"

She pulled away, laughed and went running back down the beach. Stuart gave a shout of laughter and ran after her.

Years later, she could still draw a smile from him when she reminded him of that bright, sweet morning on a Jamaican beach, when their lives together were just beginning. It was, she thought, the best morning of her life.

Center Point Publishing
600 Brooks Road ● PO Box 1
Thorndike ME 04986-0001 USA

(207) 568-3717

US & Canada:
1 800 929-9108
www.centerpointlargeprint.com